Chapter One

I was only out of my room for two minutes, I swear it. But when I got back, there she was.

A baby.

Lying there on my duvet, crying her head off.

A real, true-life baby. Come from nowhere.

I stood there, staring at her, with my brain jammed. Shaking my head. Opening and closing my eyes.

Oh my GOD! Where had she popped up from?

Was she a *ghost*?

But she didn't look like one – she was proper

pink and gurgly like a normal baby. And she wasn't wearing a flowy, ghosty cloak – she had on a real baby suit with a big red raspberry on the front.

I reached out towards her. I was thinking: *will my hand go straight through her?* I poked her quickly in the tummy. She felt solid, squidgy and warm. Definitely not made of cold cloud like ghosts.

I got even closer. Bent right over her.

She smelt sort of nice, like vanilla ice cream. She looked right back at me, with ginormous eyes full of tears. She stopped wailing the moment she saw me, and made a *cooee* baby noise. That did it – I ran backwards out of my room, tripping over the stuff on my floor.

'MUM-M-M-M!' I yelled.

Then I remembered that Mum'd gone out. Out looking for Scott AGAIN. Even though he didn't want to be her dumb boyfriend any more.

No good me calling for her.

Not now she's basically forgotten she has a daughter . . .

Little

Céleste

Dawn McNiff

HOT
KEY

For my ow... ... *and Lola xxx*

...blished in Great Britain in 2014 by Hot Key Books
No...urgh House, 1... Northburgh street, London... 0AT

Text copyright © ...

© Jan Bielecki 2014

A CIP catalogue record for this book is available from the British Library.

ISBN: 978-1-4714-0242-5

1

This book is typeset in 11.75pt Sabon using Atomik ePublisher
Printed and bound by Clays Ltd, St Ives Plc

FSC

Hot Key Books supports the Forest Stewardship Council (FSC),
the leading international forest certification organisation, and is committed to
printing only on Greenpeace-approved FSC-certified paper.
www.hotkeybooks.com

Hot Key Books is part of the Bonnier Publishing Group
www.bonnierpublishing.com

I was on my own in the house. At least I'd thought I was . . . UNTIL A BABY SUDDENLY APPEARED ON MY BED!

But babies don't just turn up on their own, do they? Or go wriggling off on their nappy bums into strange people's houses? Had someone brought her in?

I ran to the front door.

It was locked.

I ran back to the kitchen. The back door was locked and bolted. And all the windows were shut. No one could have got in.

Still, I checked in every room. I tiptoed up and down the stairs, peeking round all the doors, behind chairs and cupboards, hardly breathing, my skin all goosebumpy. It's a small house so there weren't many hiding places.

There was definitely nobody there.

It was just me and the weirdo baby.

I was kind of scared and not scared at the same time. Because she wasn't really a scary thing, being that titchy and babyish. So I went back to my bedroom door and peered round.

She was sucking her tiny thumb, happy as anything now.

I went in and crept a bit nearer.

'How'd you get in here, little frog?' I whispered. I stroked her face with the tip of my finger, and her skin felt as soft as marshmallows. 'Who's your mummy, eh?'

Oh God, it isn't Mum's, is it?

My tummy turned.

No!

Of course I knew I was being daft. There was no way Mum could've had a secret baby without me knowing. She had a dead flat tummy because she only ate get-skinny food – so obviously I would've noticed if she'd had a baby-belly sticking out under her skimpy tops.

But where on earth *had* the baby come from? It was like she'd just dropped out of the sky onto my duvet from nowhere.

Like magic.

Magic!

I got freaked out again then. It was all too loopy. I leapt off the bed away from her. I had no blinking idea what to do. All I could think of was showing her to Mum when she came back from stalking Scott.

Scott the Toadstool. That's what I called him behind his hairy back, because he smelt of disgusting, gone-off mushrooms. And he was always dead narky with me – but only on the sly when Mum couldn't hear.

I was glad glad glad he had gone, hopefully forever this time. Because now maybe me and Mum could be just the two of us – like we were when Toadstool went on a boys' night out, and she curled up in my bed with me to watch a funny film. Or even better, like we were when I was little, before she'd even met Scott. When it was just me and her all the LOVELY time . . .

Except Mum wasn't glad he'd gone.

She's turned to mush without him.

The baby was wriggling and kicking her legs about. I put pillows along the edge of the bed, just in case she roly-polied off and bumped her head. I knew normal babies did stuff like that, so maybe a magic one might too.

Then I squeezed my bum onto my windowsill. I could keep an eye on Babyface from there, and watch out for Mum.

I stared down at the traffic below, scoffing jelly babies. It was getting dark out, so I could see my blurry reflection in the window. I frowned. Mum was so pretty, but not me. I reckoned I took after our cat, Fuzz-wuzz – kind of squish-faced and wiggy.

Please come home and help me . . .

I kept looking over at the tiny thing. She'd fallen asleep – I could hear her soft, whispery breaths. Sometimes I tried tricking her – glancing away, and then back really fast to see if she disappeared. But she kept on being there.

I half wished Lexi was in too, because she always knew what to do about everything– she was a bit bossy like that. But of course she was in Ibiza, lucky her. And anyway, she'd kind of gone off with Sophie Briggs at the end of term, and started leaving me out . . .

I didn't really care.

Well, only a bit . . .

Sigh.

Still no Mum.

Before Scott went, she'd have fussed me into bed by this time – in between cooking his stupid tea, of course. She'd have nagged me to clean my teeth . . . kissed me goodnight . . . *Not just ignored me . . .*

The window was getting all steamed up, so I rubbed away a peephole with my sleeve. I could see some faint twinkles in the sky above the sea. I drew a picture of the baby on the steamy glass and made two of the little stars into her eyes.

Angel baby.

Mia and Chanel walked past in the street below, wearing identical pink hoodies. I quickly hid behind my curtain.

Ugh . . .

Bad luck for me they were starting Wirthing Secondary soon too. Brainbox Lexi had got in to the girls' High School. And Sophie Briggs had. But not me.

New horrid GROSS school in three weeks, two days . . .

By myself.

Ugh again.

I didn't mean to, but I said 'UGH' out loud. It startled the baby, and she did a lying-down starfish jump in her sleep. I clamped my hand over my mouth. I didn't want her to wake up, no way.

Oh, come on, Mum!

Maybe she isn't coming back . . .

I shook that thought out of my head. Of course she was . . .

Not that I knew what I was going to say when she did come home.

Like: 'Hello. By the way, you know you've lost the total plot since Scott left you on Saturday. Well, now I've gone mad too, because I think I've got a magic baby on my bed.'

It was all double, triple, raspberry-ripple loony.

Chapter Two

The phone went.

It wasn't Mum.

It was her boss at the hotel asking why she hadn't been to her receptionist job. She hadn't even rung in.

'She's a bit poorly,' I lied. 'Bad tummy – you know, a sicky thing.'

Sick in the head more like. Gone off her rocker over pointless Scott.

It was gone nine by the time I heard the door. Babyface was still kipping, and I was nearly dropping off myself, just sitting there waiting.

I didn't go downstairs straight off. I stayed on the windowsill and drew fast swirls in the steam until the glass squeaked.

Then I reached for the baby, holding my breath, and picked her up, dead awkward-like. She felt like a dough dolly, warm and damp and floppy. Her head lolled forward and I caught it, but she stayed asleep.

I carried her down the stairs – like a plate of dinner, all out the front.

Mum was sat on the sofa, ogling her phone. She'd kicked off her high heels into a heap – not put them back all super-tidy in the cupboard like she usually did.

She was prettied up in her best black dress. Even though it was a Tuesday night.

She glanced up. Her eyes were red and puffy, and her face looked blotchy.

Has she been crying?

My belly flipped.

Mum, like, never cries . . .

She was gibbering at me.

'Sorry I was so long, babe, but I couldn't find him again.' Her voice wobbled. 'Looked in both pubs, and sent him loads of texts, but he didn't show. No one's seen him – or his van.' She sighed and shook her head. 'He's dodging me.'

She was looking at me. Looking straight at me. And at the baby.

'Mum.' I walked over to her. 'Mum, lookie what I've got.'

It sounded dim, that: 'lookie'. I said it in a bright, fun voice like I was showing her an interesting beetle or a cake I'd made. God, even my voice was going strange now, as well.

'Mum?'

'What, darlin'?' she said. She was prodding her phone with a long nail. Probably texting Toadstool again.

'No, Mum . . . LOOK!' I practically stuffed the baby in her face. 'Baby!'

She looked. 'What? What you on about, Shelley?'

The baby was almost in her lap. She was staring right, right, right at her, but Mum flipping well couldn't see her. She really truly couldn't see her.

I was really scared then. I got pins and needles and my head started spinning. I swayed and staggered forward a step and somehow managed to knock Mum's phone out of her hands. It crashed flat on its face onto the wooden floor.

'Oh, for pity's sake, Shell!' Mum squeaked in a panic. 'If you've broken my screen . . .' She snatched up her phone like she'd die without it. She sighed. 'No, it's OK . . . phew . . .'

I opened my mouth to try once more.

Please Mum . . . switch on your eyes.

But she just half glanced up and tutted.

'Bed now please, Shell. Be my good girl and go straight up. I'll come and say night-night in a bit.'

I went. Like her good girl.

Carried the baby back upstairs, my legs wobbling.

I put her down on my bed and sat right on the other end away from her, breathing hard. She woke up and started whimpering.

Come on, Shells, pull yourself together.

My head whizzed.

Oh my God! Mum couldn't see the baby. She actually couldn't.

I turned on my big light, so I wasn't so scared. I stared at her again. Looked at her really properly this time.

She was so tiny – almost as small as a baby doll. Was it me, or was she way smaller than normal babies? And she had these strange eyes. They were pale purple like lavender flowers. Beautiful. I'd never seen eyes like that before in my whole, entire life. Lavender eyes.

I caught my breath.

Blimey, maybe she's a fairy baby!

Then I almost laughed my head off at myself. A fairy baby! I was losing it now. But secretly, I kind of hoped it might be true.

I shuffled up the bed nearer her. Gently I unpopped her suit. I slid my hand in, feeling her back for wings. Totally loony tunes, I know.

No wings.

Shame . . .

Just a dinky baby back. All soft and weeny.

Her ears were normal too – small, pink and

round. Not pointy. If she was a baby fairy or a pixie, they would be a bit pointy, wouldn't they? Maybe . . .

She started squeaking right then. Her face went all red. One second later, I had to hide my nose in my sleeve. What a right old pong and a half! She'd gone and done a poop in her nappy, and she smelt real, all right. I didn't think ghosts and fairies usually went around pooping at people. Or did they? Well, I didn't know.

She arched her back and bleated louder.

Now what am I supposed to do with a magic baby who's mucked her nappy?

Then suddenly I knew.

Brainwave.

I opened my cupboard and grabbed a stuffed-full carrier bag. Mum had tidied my room the other week and bagged up all my too-babyish tat for the charity shop. I rummaged through the bag. I knew what I was looking for. My old baby doll, Kylie.

I tugged her out. She was still a bit sticky from where I'd fed her dunked Jammy Dodgers a few summers ago. But she had these cool nappies, which were exactly like real ones but smaller. Perfect size for Little Miss Fairy. I could use one to change her tiny bum.

Then for the stinky bit.

I went to the bathroom and got some wet bog roll. Slowly, I took off her suit – it was tricky because her fingers stuck out all spiky and got in the way. She got in a right paddy. Her rubbery little legs kicked about, her face went red like a squashed raspberry, and she screamed her head off. I waited, ready for Mum to come up and see what all the racket was about, but she never did.

And she hasn't even come to say goodnight, like she promised.

'Oh well, little frog,' I said to her, 'seems like Mum can't see you *or* hear you.' It was proper weird.

Maybe she's just too busy crying herself to turn her ears on.

God, I didn't even know why she cared so much about Toadstool! She was so pretty and young, and he was hairy-bum-faced and ancient. She reckoned he was sweet to her sometimes – like sending her the odd suck-up, cheesy card. But really he just treated her like his little maidy-servant. Honestly, he walked about like he was the king or something. Getting us to bring him his tea and beer. Expecting Mum to do all his whiffy washing and cook him fry-ups that she didn't even like.

Ugh, I don't even want to think about stupid him.

I got busy with the baby again. I cleaned up her bott, and put on the clean nappy and her raspberry suit. It took ages to get all the poppers done up right. Then I put some of my doll's little booties on her too – just for cuteness.

I jiggled her in my arms and soon she stopped bleating.

'Well done, baby woo,' I said to her, kissing her little nose. 'Nice clean bott now.'

I didn't know what to do with the whiffy nappy, so in the end I stuck it in a plackie bag and hung it out of my window on the latch.

I was well proud of myself. I'd done my first nappy. *Look at me, Mini-Mum.* I was kind of getting used to her by then. Kind of. When I didn't think about her being a mad, magic baby.

I lay down and cuddled her. It was so lovely and cosy. She was gulping softly, and still had teardrops on her long, baby lashes. Then suddenly she gave me a little, wet smile.

Like I'm her own mummy.

I kissed her and began humming to her gently.

What IS that tune?

Of course! It was 'Silent Night'. Mum used to sing it to me as a lullaby – even though she didn't know the words, and it was supposed to be just for Chrimbo.

That was years ago when I was a titch.

In the good old days when it was just me and Mum. Before I had to share her.

'Silent Night, hole in your tights. All is calm, all is bright . . .'

I sang and hummed it over and over. It was a funny old church song, but soothing somehow.

Soon the baby dropped off, tucked up against my tummy like a small, fat teddy bear.

'Where did you come from, Fairycake?' I

whispered. 'I just don't get it, but I'm so glad you came.'

We stayed all curled up together for hours. We heard Mum come up. She stopped outside my door like she was listening. But she didn't come in and just scuffed off to bed, sniffing.

I sighed and quickly hugged the baby closer. We listened to faraway seagulls and the rain plinking at the windows. It was so snuggly, just the two of us. She sucked her thumb and dozed on and off, but of course there was no way I could sleep. I was too wowed by her.

Then suddenly I knew her name. It just pinged into my head.

'Celeste,' I whispered to her. 'That's what I'm calling you. It's a magic name – for proper girl angels.' She peeped up at me then, and I swear her lavender eyes glittered like fairy lights in the greyness. Like she had real stars for eyes.

So maybe she was a real baby fairy then. Maybe she COULD do magic and grant wishes.

I know what I'd wish for . . .

I wondered if it was mean to make a wish.

She was only a baby so she might not know any magic yet.

I decided to start with an easy wish that would only need a little spell.

'I wish for . . . um . . . um . . .' My brain was concrete.

'I wish for . . . um . . . some bubblegum. Cherry cola flavour, please!'

I looked at her and waited. Celeste sucked her thumb and looked back at me blankly.

'But it doesn't matter if you can't though!' I said, quickly.

I was hoping my room would suddenly be piled high with bubblegum packets, like a tipper truck had just emptied itself through the window.

But nothing happened.

I felt dumb then.

'Never mind,' I said. I kissed her soft head. 'Magic is very hard.'

But I still made a bigger wish, quietly in my head.

Please make Mum turn back into Mum, and remember about me again.

Chapter Three

Mum was so small she could sit in Toadstool's hand. He stuffed her in his footie practice bag, zipped it up and ran to the door.

'No, give her back!' I yelled, furiously. 'You can't have her. No! Mum! Mummm!'

I jerked out of my dream, and wiped my wet face on my duvet cover.

'NO! NO, MAMA!' The crying went on. 'MAMAAA!'

Not my voice. A baby voice.

I turned over, and my nose stuffed up against

a bottom. A big bottom in a fat nappy.

I jolted upright and stared. I lay down again and blinked a lot through my tears.

Maybe I am still asleep.

I shook my head. No, I WAS awake. And it really was true: I had a chubby baby sat on my pillow. A great BIG baby.

'MAAA!' she screeched in fury.

Crying her bonce off . . . for her mum . . .

Just like I was.

'MAA?' She looked down at me with huge baby eyes full of tears.

It was Celeste.

I'd have known those cutie lavender eyes anywhere. But she was loads bigger. She was not quite a toddler, but certainly a crawler. And a wriggler. And a shouter. Her hair was longer too, golden and wavy, and swept around her head in a Mr Whippy whirl.

She'd grown months in one single night.

Oh my God!

My mind went woozy and black for a minute – like when you hang upside down on a climbing frame for too long. My hands went shaky and my skin prickled. That decided it, then. I'd lost my marbles completely. Maybe I really did need a head doctor. Maybe I had to tell Mum.

Except Mum was too busy losing her own marbles over Scott. And she'd never believe me.

I could hardly believe it myself really. But there she was – larger than life, and definitely larger than yesterday.

'MAMAMA,' she wailed, throwing herself on top of me.

'I know,' I whispered, hugging her close to me. 'Do you need your mama too?' I stroked her back, and snuggled her, humming soft songs. Slowly her screeching calmed to little gulps. And then all of sudden, she sat up and gave me a great big drooly grin.

'Ogggg!' she squealed and blew a wet raspberry at me.

'Oh, did the sun come out?' I smiled.

She clapped her hands, and crawled round the bed, cooing, chattering and chirping away to herself, with her nappy hanging heavy inside her suit.

I just lay there, gawping at her, trying to get my head on straight.

What is going on?

It was the strangest thing . . . that little face. It was almost like I knew her. But how could I? I didn't know any babies – except Laura Mead's little brother, and he was a boy, and about two or something.

She seemed quite happy with me now, anyhow. She pulled my cheeks around like play dough and tangled her fingers up in my hair until it was one big knot. She gave me lots of loud, sloppy kisses and blinked up at me prettily through her long eyelashes. Extra-long dark eyelashes. Just like Mum's . . .

I stared at her hard.

Like Mum's . . . ?

And what was that suit she was wearing? Where had it come from? It had little rabbits all over it – I felt like I'd seen that before somewhere too, but I didn't know where.

It was so weird my brain was mushing.

But Celeste didn't give me a chance to be freaked out for long. She sat on top of me, hugged me round my neck, nearly strangling me, and jogged up and down.

'Clip clop clip clop!' she clicked.

'Oh, you want to play horsies.' I swung my legs over the edge of my bed and sat her across my lap. I held her little hands, and we galloped until she had hiccups from laughing so much.

'God, don't be sick,' I panted. 'Hey, do you know any other animals? What noise does a duck make?'

A big smile spread over her face.

'Wack, wack, wack,' she quacked, dead pleased with herself – like she'd just answered the winning question on *Who Wants to Be a Millionaire?*

'Whoa, clever clogs!' I was amazed she knew. Someone must have taught her. Her fairy mum?

Then I thought maybe they had different animals in fairyland. Of course they did – anyone knew that.

'What noise does a . . . er . . . unicorn make?' I asked her. She looked at me blankly.

'Woof?' she said, hopefully.

'Never mind, my cherub,' I said. Although actually I was a teeny bit disappointed because I'd hoped I'd find out some fairyland secrets from her.

She grabbed my teddy and started gnawing his ear. It looked like it was time for her breakfast – and it was nearly nine already.

I plonked her on my bedroom floor and let her crawl around.

'Be good!' I whispered. 'I'll be back in a jiff with some yum-yum for your tum-tum.'

Mum used to call it that when I was little.

I tiptoed down to the kitchen. Blimey, what a mess. The sink was still full of burnt-on pans from the last sausage dinner Mum'd cooked for Toadstool. A huge mountain of dirty washing sat by the washing machine. I had never seen the house look this grimy before. It was like it wasn't my house. Or rather, not Mum's house. Mum the neat-freak who irons socks, and has a hoover as a pet.

Used to.

Before she went gaga.

I sighed. Mum's neat-freaking usually got on my nerves. But now I actually wished she would be like it again. Be her normal self again . . .

No time to think about that. I had a hungry baby to feed. I stared into the cupboard. I knew babies ate banana, so I grabbed one, and a bowl and fork for mashing it . . .

I heard a noise in the front room.

Was Mum up?

But it was just our cat, Fuzz-wuzz, scratching the sofa. Or I should say Scott's cat, because she only liked him now. He was dead soft on her too – they were like a hairy little married couple.

It didn't matter what Fuzz-wuzz did. She didn't even get in trouble when she pooed in his shoe. But me, I couldn't breathe without him snarling at me behind Mum's back. And when Mum wasn't there, he always sent me to my room for absolute nothing.

Hope he's missing Fuzz-wuzz and crying.

Fuzz-wuzz stalked in, gave me a filthy look and shot out through her cat flap. She was always like that now – I reckon Scott'd trained her to hate me.

I crept back up the stairs, wondering why it was suddenly so quiet.

I pushed open my door with my foot.

Silence.

The room was empty.

Celeste had vanished.

Chapter Four

I panicked.

I raced around my room, yanking up my covers and pulling stuff out of my cupboard at a hundred miles an hour.

Please don't be gone . . .

It was totally loony because she'd only been with me a little while, but I couldn't bear it if she was . . .

I held my breath, and gritted my teeth. Sharp pins and needles ran down me. Maybe I'd crazied out, and made Celeste up. Perhaps next

I would see giant bunnies, and talk to myself in supermarket queues like a proper maddo.

I ran to the window. The plackie bag full of dirty nappy was still dangling off the latch.

So it *had* all happened.

Then there was a squawk.

And a saggy nappy bum, reversing out from under my bed.

Celeste!

She was a bit wedged so I had to give her a pull. And she was green. All over. Her face and fingers were green. The inside of her mouth was green. Gripped in her little fist was a green felt tip.

I looked under my bed. She had drawn all over the wall. Baby graffiti.

'Oh, Celeste!' I said, weakly.

She gave me a big, wet smile, like she was super-proud.

'It's all right for you,' I said, hugging her tight. 'YOU won't get it in the neck from Mum, cos she can't see *bad* fairy babies like you. Well, I'll have to wipe it off later. First, brekkie.'

I mashed the banana while Celeste watched

with wide eyes.

'Naana bejana . . . !' she sang. She bopped on her bottom on my lap in time to her song, like she was having her own little nappy disco. 'Naana bejana! Naana bejana!' I knew what she was singing straight off – *Bananas in Pyjamas*. It was the tune from that telly programme I loved when I was small.

'YOU are a banana in pyjamas!' I said, laughing. 'Come on – open wide.'

She scoffed loads down, before lunging for the bowl, grabbing some banana gloop and blobbing it in her own hair and all over me. We were both totally plastered in it.

Celeste shrieked with laughter.

'Oh my God, Miss Happy Nappy – you are big trouble!' I said, laughing too and wiping her gooey face while she squirmed. 'What am I going to do with you now you've grown all big and cheeky-faced?'

I stood holding her up on the windowsill so she could look out. She bounced, licked the glass and shouted at the sea in joy.

The sky was dark and hanging heavy over the churning sea, and it was spitting through watery sunshine. And then . . . a rainbow stretched far across the sky. Celeste went quiet and stared. All the pinks, reds and purples shone in her eyes.

'There's fairy gold at the end of rainbows, isn't there, pixie?' I whispered to her. 'Did you hide your baby fairy pocket money at the end of one? Lend us some squids, eh? I need it to buy YOU some big-girl nappies.' Her nappy was now so baggy it was nearly round her knees.

I had no idea how I was going to manage nappy-shopping. First problem, no money. Second, what to do with Celeste. I couldn't leave her at home, obviously, because she would get up to too much baby badness – but how was I going to carry her now she was such a lumpster? I needed one of those baby carriers I'd seen in town, so I could lug her on my back.

Then I had an idea.

I found my old rucksack, and cut some leg holes in the bottom. I gently wriggled Celeste into it, while she giggled away and tried to poke her fingers up my nose as I leant over her.

I somehow hauled her onto my back. She was a right heffalump, and her pudgy legs dangled right down to my knees, but I could just manage. She was made up, and whooped right in my earhole.

There. We were sorted and ready to go out.

Except for the money.

I still had £2 of last year's birthday money left, but of course that wasn't going to be enough. There was nothing for it – I'd have to borrow some of Mum's . . . I would pay her back.

Mum was still in bed. I could see her through the crack in the door, all lumped up under her duvet. Her room looked like a jumble sale. None of her normal perfect piles. She'd usually hoovered and bleached the whole of Lunham by this time of the morning, but it looked as if she was getting in a few more hours of moping about Scott instead. Like the whole of the week.

Sniff.

Is she crying AGAIN?

Mum, like, never cries. I only saw her cry once, when I rode my bike over her toe.

35

Sniff, sniff.

My heart started galloping. Celeste wriggled and grumbled on my back.

I couldn't cope if Mum was blubbing.

I staggered as fast as I could down the stairs, and swiped a handful of change from Mum's bag in the hall. I would never have dared usually – never! I was always such a goody-goody girl. But we needed nappies – and badly. And somehow having Celeste with me made me feel braver . . .

I was making for the back door – but then something caught my eye.

I stopped.

There was a piece of bubblegum on the hall windowsill.

I grabbed it before Celeste could, unwrapped it and chewed. Cherry cola flavour.

Exactly what I'd wished for last night.

Weird . . .

I hadn't bought any of that for ages. And it wasn't Mum's – she only had sugar-free gum.

So had my little wish come true?

Had Celeste magicked the gum?

I twisted my head round to look at her. But she was just sat there, sucking her podgy thumb like nothing had happened.

Chewing on my gum – *my magic gum?* – I waddled down the garden path and through the back gate.

Chapter Five

I walked down the back lane. It was drizzling a bit, and I wondered if Celeste would be cold in her babygro thingy. But she just seemed proper chuffed with her high-up seat on my back. She shouted 'OOO!' at the trees and 'MAAAA!' at the sky. She chuckled, cooed and sang, loud and happy. She'd got a big gob, all right. Not like her shy mum.

That's me, her new mum. Kind of.

As we got to the corner I saw three people at the bus stop.

Then I had a mad idea: I could check if the bus people could see Celeste. Because what if it was just Mum being dense and not making her eyes work? And it wasn't like I had to worry – I didn't know any of them, and what were they going to do anyway? Point and scream and phone the fairy police? No, if they could see her, they'd think Celeste was my baby sister, that was all.

I queued next to them, all casual like. Celeste burbled and chattered. I felt like I was standing on a stage in the nuddy with all the spotlights on me, but no one took any notice of us at all.

I walked on.

My test hadn't really worked. Maybe the bus people had seen Celeste, but thought she was just any old baby.

Not a magic one . . .

Celeste was kicking her legs into my sides like she was riding a fat pony, and yanking hard at my banana-y hair. I couldn't help squealing, which made her laugh and pull even harder. She bounced and swayed in her seat so much, I had a job staying upright. I kept walking like I'd been at

Toadstool's beer. It was lucky there was no one about for once.

'Bum!' shrieked Celeste. She lunged at a stripy cat sitting on a wall.

What?

'Bum!' She hung out of her seat, her fat little fingers stretched towards the cat.

'Not "bum",' I laughed. 'CAT.'

'Bum!' she said, firmly. 'BUM!' Well, at least it was a real word, I thought, in a proud mum-ish way. Even if it was a bit rude and not right.

'You want to see the nice pussy cat?' I said. 'C-a-t . . . CAT.' I crouched down so she could get a good look at him.

'Bum! Bum!'

Why does she call cats Bum?

'OK, you win, you mini muppet,' I laughed. 'Blinking "bum" it is.' Maybe that's what cats were called in Fairyland.

We stayed ages stroking Bum-cat. I had to crouch down side-on to the wall so she could reach him too. He purred and purred, and Celeste squealed and squealed. Then I had a thought.

Can Bum-cat see Celeste?

I pulled my hand away. Celeste carried on stroking Bum-cat – but in a hard, bangy way. He jumped down and ran away into someone's garden. Could he feel her patting and stroking? Had she made him go? It was hard to tell without talking Cat Talk.

My shoulders ached like mad. But when I tried to walk on Celeste had a paddy. She arched backwards in the rucksack so I nearly fell over, and screamed. She didn't want to leave her Bum-cat.

'Look, you baby troll,' I said, crossly, 'time to go!' And I just walked and let her bawl. A man went past, but he didn't seem to notice the terrible din.

I tried blowing some bubblegum bubbles to entertain her. I turned my head so she could see. Each time one popped, she nearly jumped in the air, and squealed laughing.

'Pop!' I said.

'Pop! POP!' she shouted.

Then I blew a really good one. I kept blowing – bigger, bigger, BIGGER . . .

'Pop?' she yelled impatiently. 'PO-O-O-P!' She swiped at me with her little mitt. The bubble burst and the gum stuck to her hand.

'Pop,' she said in a small, sad voice.

And grabbed my hair with her gummed-up fingers.

The gum stuck in my hair in a thick lump. I tugged and tugged at it, but it was completely gooed in. Great – now I had to go in the shop looking like that.

'Oh, now look what you've done!' I said it a bit gruffly. Then I felt bad because she started blubbing, so I found half a biscuit in my other pocket and handed it to her. She grabbed it, and I guessed she was sucking it because she went all quiet.

Celeste loved the shop and cheered up no end. No one took any notice of us again – just like at the bus stop. The only person I recognised was Kieran Lawn from Year Five's mum – and she didn't look at me. Which was lucky because Celeste was bouncing up and down so fast, she was bouncing me too. I tried to walk all normal but I couldn't. So I walked up the pasta aisle in time to her bounces, in a dancing-and-whistling way, like shopping in the Co-op made me feel happy, happy, happy.

Then, from her high seat, Celeste swiped at a shelf. I wasn't quick enough and she got her chubby mitts on a huge bottle of olive oil.

And dropped it.

Chapter Six

It smashed.

Celeste screamed, nearly pulling me over backwards as she leant out to see where the bottle had gone. Everyone stared, until a Co-op shop-girl appeared, glaring, She had purple hair and an eyebrow ring, and looked like she hated her life, but most of all me.

Of course I had to act like I'd dropped it. I didn't think she would buy any A-Magic-Baby-Did-It stories.

'Sorry,' I said as sweetly as I could, but she just

cracked her gum and made a face at the greasy, glassy mess.

Then Celeste took her chance and grabbed at the girl's shiny eyebrow ring.

'NO!' I yelled and jumped back, but her stubby fingers brushed the end of the shop girl's nose.

'No, no, no!' Celeste raged, banging her hands on my head like a drum.

'What the—!' The girl was scowling and rubbing her nose.

'Sorry!' I squeaked. 'I caught you with my . . . er . . . rucksack.'

She gave me a death stare through her eyeliner.

'Just go,' she said. 'Move it! I'll have to tell the manager.' She turned to walk off, but . . .

'WAAAAA!' screeched Celeste, reaching for her again. She was mad for that dippy eyebrow ring. 'WAAAA!'

'No, shhhhhh!' I said, before I could stop myself.

'You what?' said the girl, whirling round. 'You giving me lip too?'

'No, no . . . sorry, really!' I pulled up my hood

and scarpered to the next aisle, feeling hot and bothered. I needed to get out of there soon before Celeste got me locked up.

Quick as I could I found the baby section and just grabbed stuff – a pack of nappies, a baby bottle, some baby milk cartons. That would be all my birthday money gone. And all Mum's money gone.

Hope she doesn't realise. She'll be so shocked at me . . . I queued up at the till. Celeste was fidgeting and whining – I looked around to see if anyone was looking at us. But no one was.

Oi, Lunham dimbos, fairy baby here. Can't you see?

Nah?

But my face was still burning up, standing there holding baby stuff. What if the queue people thought I was, like, a teenage mum buying nappies? Ugh! No, they couldn't think that – I looked way too small and young. I was eleven, but I only looked about nine.

There was a new man on the till – I'd never seen him before. It said MARK WHITESON – SHOP

MANAGER on his badge. He was really nice about me wrecking his shop.

'You been having a smashing time?' he said with a wink.

'Mmm,' I stammered. 'Sorry.'

'No worries!' he said cheerfully. 'Accidents happen.'

Celeste seemed to like him too. She started cooing cutely, but he didn't blink an eye.

He handed me the nappies.

'You got a little brother or sis, then?' he asked.

I felt myself go even redder. I nodded shyly. Big, fat lie, but what else could I say?

'That's cool,' he said. 'I . . .' He stopped mid-sentence and gave my hair an odd look. I put my hand up to touch it. Yukko. The lump of gum was still there. And lots of spat-out biscuit – like huge, damp bits of dandruff.

Great – now even the Nice New Manager Man thinks I'm a mentalist.

I paid and, without waiting for my penny change, made for the door, brushing the crumbs out of my hair . . .

But as I passed the newspaper rack, my tummy did a head-over-heels.

In big letters across the front of a paper, it said: *LOCAL COUPLE'S BABY AGONY.*

Chapter Seven

I pushed in front of a man reading the sports. He tutted loudly, but for once I couldn't have cared less. I held the paper away from Celeste's grabby fingers, and my eyes flew down the page.

Baby this, baby that. My brain tried to make sense of the words. Then I got it. The story was about an ill baby who needed expensive medicine.

It was not about a lost baby.

It was not about Celeste.

Yes!

It was silly, but I was so glad Celeste wasn't

somebody else's lost baby. I just wanted her to be my own magic one – there was no way I wanted to give her up now. And anyway, she needed me, didn't she . . . to be her new mum.

Oh, Mum . . .

I pushed the sad thought away. There was no time to get all hopeless like Mum was. I had a baby to look after, didn't I?

Celeste was getting bored and swinging herself from side to side – and it was just then I realised that the Tutting Man was still behind me, reading the paper headlines over my shoulder. But where he was standing, it was honestly like he was reading *through* Celeste . . . I moved back a bit so Celeste was completely in front of his eyes. He tutted again, but stayed where he was and just kept on reading. Reading right through Celeste like he had X-ray eyes.

Like she isn't even there.

At that moment I knew for sure. She was really properly invisible. And see-through. No one could see her. No one but me.

Too weird, too weird!

I went goosebumpy again. I suddenly felt as if I was in one world with Celeste, and all other humans were in another world, somewhere else completely.

I want to go home . . .

I stuffed the newspaper back onto the shelf and scooted out the door not looking where I was going.

And walked straight bang-crash into a boy on a bike.

He was about my age but I'd never seen him before. Which was odd because Lunham-by-Sea was a small town, and he was a boy you would notice. He had this loud, yellow-striped, waspy bike, and too-long ginger hair which stuck up at the front so he looked like a chicken.

'Sorry.' He rolled his Wasp Bike out of my way and smiled. It was a friendly smile. Maybe he was a nice chicken-ish boy.

I smiled back, and tried to get by, but another boy lolloped over and blocked my way. Then my smile dropped straight off my face. It was Brandon from my old class, or Slugface as I called him. Except I only called him that very quietly to myself because he was a big lanky bully. Even way back in Reception his hobbies were stealing people's KitKats, eating flowers and mud, and sitting outside Mrs Green the head teacher's office.

'All right?' Brandon said to Chicken Boy, all matey. He stuffed a fistful of oniony crisps into his gob, turned to me and sneered. 'Oh, look, it's Belly.' He'd always called me that – short for Smelly Shelley Jelly-Belly. 'What you doing? Trying to make a new friendy-wendy?' He looked so pleased with himself – like he'd invented rhyming. 'Well, you got no chance. Jay's just moved to town, but lucky I know who all the girlie-losers are – ones like YOU!' He blew onion stink and wet crisp bits into my face. 'Right, Jay?'

Chicken Boy stared at the ground, his face red. 'Whatever,' he muttered.

He was a strange one. He didn't seem as horrible as Brandon the Slugface, so why was he hanging around with him?

Then I caught a glimpse of something under his chickeny sleeve . . .

What?

I couldn't believe my eyes. He had a sparkly friendship bracelet round his wrist.

A *girls'* bracelet.

How weird. But then Slugface would only get a weirdo friend. His one and only friend ever.

Celeste was wriggling madly on my back. I checked the boys' faces, but they weren't looking at her at all. I tried to get past, but Slugface stepped in my way.

Oh no, he wants to show off to his new chicken friend . . .

'So, you bought me any sweets, Bells?' he said, reaching out and flicking my tummy. 'Or you pigged them all down already?'

I shook my head, avoiding his eyes, and folding my arms over my tummy. I would never pick a fight with anyone, let alone Slugface. He'd given me too many Chinese burns in my life. I tried to go past again, but Celeste rolled in her seat, nearly tipping me off balance.

'NOOOOOOOOO!' she shouted. Right at Slugface.

Whoa, she's got proper cross all of a sudden.

'Pooooo!' she hollered. 'Poo!'

Ha, Slugface the big poo! I wish I could dare to say that . . . .

I tried to stop myself, but a tiny giggle squeaked out of me.

Mistake . . .

Slugface looked surprised, and then his eyes narrowed into a right evil look. There was no way he was going to let me get one over on him in front of his new friend.

'What you laughing at?' he spat.

'Nothing,' I said, staring at the ground.

Uh-oh, now I've done it . . .

'Hey . . . but I know what IS funny,' sneered Slugface, ' . . . your mum's boyf doing a runner!'

Uh?!

How did Slugface know about Scott leaving? God, Lunham-by-stupid-Sea was such a small town – everyone knew everything.

'Yeah, I heard my gran say.' He nudged Jay. 'I reckon he left cos Belly's too guffy – he couldn't stand the stink no more.'

My whole body went hot. Celeste yelled her head off over my shoulder, kicking her legs in rage. I wanted to stamp my feet too. I screwed up my fists and bit back my words.

Shut your face, Slugface! At least I can blinking well read!

Brandon had to have special help at school. I knew it was unkind, but I soooo wanted to say it to him. I just didn't dare. But Celeste dared. She was clawing the air towards him and bawling. 'NOOOO!'

I felt dizzy – it was all too much. I tried dodging around Slugface, but he spat on the ground and bounded after me, grabbing the nappies out of my bag.

'Mess your pants, do yer?' he laughed. He flung the fat packet at me really hard.

I fell, banging my elbow against the Co-op's automatic doors.

The doors slid open and closed, open and closed behind me.

Celeste screamed.

Oh no, Celeste!

The moody Co-op girl was suddenly at the door.

'What the hell is going on?' She took one look at me, and nearly exploded. 'You again!' she spat. 'Get lost right now! RIGHT NOW!'

I nabbed the nappies and my plackie bag of shopping out of a puddle, and legged it away while Celeste continued her screaming ab-dabs on my back.

'Belle – wait!' Chicken Boy called after me.

What? Now he's calling me that too! I hate him . . .

I looked over my shoulder. Slugface was getting an earful from the Co-op girl, but Chicken Boy was watching me go.

Oh God, are they going to come and get me?

And they had bikes. I only had my short legs.

Chapter Eight

The traffic was stopped at the lights, so I charged across the main road towards the beach. Celeste sobbed even louder as she was thrown around in her high seat. But I kept going, across the rough grass and onto the shingle, slipping and sliding on the pebbles.

'It's all right!' I called up to her as I ran.

But it wasn't. My head was banging. And I could still see Slugface's daggers look.

I was sure he was going to come after us – with his new chickeny mate – and they were going to do me in, good and proper. I tried to listen as I ran – were they coming? I couldn't hear a thing, just my own gaspy breaths.

Then I tripped and fell flat on the pebbles.

It hurt.

I stayed there for a moment on all fours squeezing my eyes shut so no tears would come out. I wanted to cry so much, but I don't do crying. Not ever, full stop. I held my breath and my nose fizzled. I could feel Celeste wriggling and boo-hooing on my back.

But what's happened to her cry? It's such a tiny bleat . . .

I staggered up and my rucksack felt oddly light. *Uh?*

I shrugged the bag off my shoulders, and there, flumped in the bottom like a little cloth doll, was Celeste. But the newborn Celeste again.

She's shrunk!

But I had no time to think. Looking over my shoulder again and still blinking back my tears, I carried on running, with the teeny, bleating Celeste bundled up inside the rucksack in my arms.

It wasn't till I got to the edge of the sea that I realised what a numpty I'd been. It was high tide, so the beach was only a skinny strip. There was nowhere to hide down there. Nowhere to go.

I turned round fast, ready to scream my block off, but the beach was empty. No boys. No one at all.

Not yet.

Could we make it over to the beach huts? I knew there was one with a kicked-in door.

I ran again, face into the sharp wind.

We dived inside the hut. It stank of old wee. The door had a huge hole in it and was hanging on one hinge, but I managed to sort of tie it up with a ripped plastic bag I found on the floor.

I hugged Celeste closer to me and stroked her soft little head. She was beside herself – crying so much she was choking on her tears and her babygro was all damp. I found an old picnic blanket from the hut cupboard, and huddled us both up in it. I sat in the half-dark and rocked her.

All the time I was peering through the hole in the door, keeping an eye out for the boys. *Nothing,*

nothing, no one. So either they hadn't come after me, or I'd lost them. I'd been running like a crazy loser girl for nothing.

But I didn't dare leave yet, just in case. So I waited, squinting out at the rain while Celeste cried and cried.

Everything on the beach looked dim and grey. Just banks of dull pebbles, litter and washed-up old breeze blocks, half chewed by the waves. Grizzly-drizzly clouds, ponky car smells from the big road, and seagulls wark-wark-warking in the sky. I couldn't even see the horizon: it was like the rain had washed the whole sky into the sea. A big downpour was coming our way.

Lovely blinking summer. Lovely Lunham-by-stupid-Sea.

Celeste snivelled on.

My eyes began stinging again. All the bad things kept churning like the sea in my brain. Enough that I could even make a sad little list in my head:

1. Mum doesn't care about me any more.
2. Mum has gone properly mad.

3. I found a magic baby on my bed, which probably means I'm mad too.

4. Slugface wants to mash me, even more than normal. And so does Chicken Boy.

5. I'm starting stupid secondary school soon. By myself.

I sucked and chewed at my sleeve until I'd made a hole

Gulping and whimpering, Celeste found her thumb. I curled up tighter around her and let myself suck my thumb too . . . even though I hadn't done it for years.

'I'm being a baby like you,' I whispered to her.

I rocked Celeste and twirled her hair. I hummed Silent Night again. She went floppier and her breathing slowed – until we were breathing together, in time, and she was asleep in my arms, warm against my tummy. Cosy and dozy – like she'd melted into me. Soft, slow breaths, seagulls, the swish, swish, swish of the sea . . .

I woke up with a start.

I was cold . . .

I knew straight off that Celeste had gone.

No . . . !

My mouth went all dry like I'd been sucking tissues, and my legs felt like jelly.

The door was still tied up but the hut was empty

Oh God, this time she really has left me.

I leapt up, pushed the door down and scanned the beach. I could see for miles. It was definitely empty. And anyway, she'd been cuddled into me a second ago. I could still feel her warmth on my tummy.

I knew I wouldn't find her, but I still galumphed up and down the beach, with my teeth chattering at the wind.

Then, right on the other side of the main road. I caught sight of a lady with a pram.

Of course it was stupid – but I walked faster. Just to double check . . .

Please let it be Celeste in there.

Chapter Nine

Still with a beady eye out for chickens and slugfaces, I followed the lady and pram into the charity shop.

The lady was damp from the rain, and smelt sweet and flowery.

Like a proper mum.

Her baby cooed, and the sound made my tummy roly-poly.

Could it be . . .?

I put on my sweet-little-girl smile.

'Can I look at your baby, please?' I asked.

'Of course.' The lady smiled back at me. 'She's just woken up.'

I held my breath for a moment and – *Oh God, here goes* – peeped in under the hood.

But the little eyes gazing up at me were navy blue, not lavender. The tufts of baby hair were dark and straight, not golden and fuzzy. I breathed again. She wasn't Celeste.

Of course not, silly.

'Ahhhh, she's so cute . . .' I said. 'How old is she?'

'Oh, she's very new. Just one week old.'

A newborn? But she was much, much bigger than Celeste had been that first day she came.

'Gosh, she's very big, isn't she?' I said.

'Not really. Below average actually.'

I moved out of her way, and found myself in front of a basket full of baby clothes. I rummaged through it, thinking about what the lady had said. So Celeste was a complete and utter titch then. Super small. And I could see that most of the baby clothes in the basket would be gigantic on her.

Small like a fairy.

The thought made me go lovely and shivery.

I wanted to buy some sweet suits for the tiny, fairy Celeste, and a rattle for the big, bad wiggly Celeste – in case either came back.

Please come back . . .

But I'd spent all Mum's money and all my birthday money.

Birthday . . .

Mum . . .

Then I remembered . . .

It was actually Mum's birthday TODAY, and I'd gone and forgotten. Celeste coming had made it fall out of my head.

I dashed out of the shop, feeling proper mean. I always try and make a Special Birthday Fuss of her and make her Birthday Brekkie, three or four cards, and buy her bath bubbles or something. Because obviously Toadstool never bothers. Mum reckons he bought her flowers one year, but I expect he just nicked them from the park.

I sprinted it home.

'Hello!' I called out, bursting through the back door.

No answer.

It was way after lunch.

Surely Mum isn't still in bed?

I stood on the doormat, biting my lip, looking around at the still-super-messy kitchen. My eyes fell on the faded, framed photo of me and Mum that'd hung for years by the door. It was the only one in the house, because Mum didn't like things that caught the dust. But I'd always loved it . . . I was holding a wonky cake we'd made, and we were both grinning our heads off. Best of all, I was about five which meant Toadstool hadn't wormed along yet to totally ruin everything.

I sighed.

But where IS Mum?

I crossed the kitchen and opened the door. There was a funny noise coming from upstairs. I crept to the bottom of the stairs and listened.

It was Mum in her room, singing along to the radio.

Wailing out some soft heartbreak song.

I climbed the stairs two at a time

Her bedroom door was open. She'd stopped

singing and was sat on her bed with her head in her hands. She looked so thin that one flick would break her into lots of pieces. She had on her jeans, bra and one sock – like she'd stopped halfway through dressing.

She's even starting to look like a nutter now.

She sighed.

And sniffed.

Was she crying?

My throat went tight.

Quickly I turned to go, but the floorboard creaked

Mum jumped off the bed, like she had ice down her back.

'Who's that?' she squeaked.

'Just Shelley,' I said.

Your daughter, remember.

'Oh, Shells, darling, I thought you were . . .' Her voice trailed off, but I knew she'd thought I was Toadstool.

Wished.

'No, it's only me,' I muttered. 'Soz . . .'

Sorry not to be a gross gorilla. Who you seem

to love more than me.

'I just wanted to say Happy Birthday,' I said. I tried to sound bright and birthday-ish, but it didn't work.

She rubbed her face hard with her palms. 'Yeah . . . course, thanks. Happy Birthday to me.' She did a high, pretend laugh. 'Happy, happy!'

'Mum, really,' I said, 'you can be the Birthday Princess and I'll be your lady. Yeah?'

I curtsied and started singing Happy Birthday at the top of my best toady voice.

I didn't know why I was banging on – I just so wanted her to stop looking grim.

Whatever you do, don't cry more. Please.

'Sorry, sweet,' she said, stopping me before I'd even got to the squashed tomatoes bit. 'Got a headache. And I'm just not in a birthday mood really.'

'But I got you a pressie,' I lied. 'Wait there!'

I flew back to my room and rummaged through a drawer. I found a small soap I'd got in a party bag once – it was shaped like a cat except one ear had fallen off. I stuffed it in a paper bag, ran and handed it to Mum.

She opened it slowly and looked in.

'Um . . . it's kind of a joke present,' I said, my face going hot. 'For the loo basin.'

'Right,' she said. 'Ta, darling.' She squeezed my hand and tried to smile, but her face just twisted. For a moment her eyes met mine.

Mum . . .

'Look, Shell, sorry, eh . . .' she said, softly. 'None of this is your fault, my love.'

My throat went into a tight ball. I wanted to dive into her arms.

But her eyes were glancing down again at her phone. I could see the screen was blank. No message.

And I knew it was a bad thing to say even as it was coming out of my mouth.

'Mum, please . . . we don't need him!'

Big mistake.

'But *I* need him!' Her eyes filled with tears. 'So much . . . I just don't know what to do with myself without him.'

She coughed and gulped. I knew she was fighting

to hold some big crying in. With shaking hands, she tidied the dirty wine glasses on her bedside table. She lined them up straight, in a perfect line.

Then with a deep breath, she got up. She kissed me on the cheek and went downstairs, dragging her duvet behind her. I followed her down.

She grabbed a glass of water, put the telly on to any old thing, and curled up under her duvet on the sofa.

'Soz, babe – I'm just going to have another nap.' She closed her eyes, hugging her phone like it was a teddy.

At least she's not crying any more.

There was no room for me on the sofa, so I just sat on the floor with the telly on quiet, watched junk and chomped through another whole bag of jelly babies.

The rain banged on and on at the windows.

I made Mum some lemon curd on toast cut into a heart shape, and put it next to her.

She did wake up once. She just stared at her blank phone screen again, and then with a big, sad sigh, turned over and went back to sleep. She hadn't even noticed her heart toast.

I may as well be invisible.

I went to my room to check if Celeste had abracadabra-ed herself back onto my bed.

Please be there. Just for one hug . . .

But she wasn't.

I hung out of my window and stared out over the rough sea.

I started to think maybe Celeste really was never *ever* coming back.

And Mum's going to be bleak and mental forever.

My throat went hard and tight again. So I played a game of trying to count to ten between gull squawks. I told myself if I did it, things would get nicer.

But I only ever counted to seven. The gulls were too gobby.

Chapter Ten

Mum . . .

Mum . . .

She was there in my room. Smiling. Happy. Reaching for me. I fought to sit up, to reach back to her . . .

I woke up.

I was gasping for breath. Something heavy . . . on my chest . . .

Celeste!

Teeny-weeny Celeste. Like the first time she came.

She was gulping and gasping too. Like she was going to cry and cry and cry forever. I breathed deeply and swallowed hard. I stroked her head to soothe her.

Oh, she's back! At last.

I squeezed and snuffled her to make sure she was still the same Celeste. She had that same strange, nice, sweet smell – kind of like vanilla ice cream – and she felt as warm and squidgy as ever. I couldn't believe she was there – back from nowhere. A mini miracle.

We lay in the early morning light – for how long, I wasn't sure. I just held her close to me.

'Don't leave me again!' I whispered. It felt nicer when she was there. Somehow she just magicked everything a bit better.

She was a little handful though. What a mini monkey. I got up and tried to get dressed. But she was only happy if I carried her around the whole, complete and utter time. If I put her down on my bed for even half a millisecond, she started squeaking. And it was the saddest sound ever, and made me think of baby Dumbo, when he's all alone and mum-less. I couldn't bear it, so I had to hoick her right back up again.

I didn't know if all babies were such little cling-ons. Or was it just that Celeste was starving hungry for cuddles? Or missing her fairy mum? *Bit like me.*

Then Celeste spotted a gull out of the window. And screamed. She was totally terrified.

'Oh Celeste – you are such a copycat,' I laughed. I hated gulls too – they gave me the shivers. 'You're like a mini me.' I shut the curtains on the gull, and tried giving her my doll's dummy. But she gobbed it out and kept on crying louder and louder: *WA WA WA WA*, like a police car.

'It's OK, scaredy-kitten. The nasty gull has gone.' I tried dancing around the room in a posh *Strictly Come Dancing* style with her held against me. I tried singing to her, but she just cried on and on, chewing her teeny fist, sucking my nightie and bawling. There was nothing I could do and I was getting a bit stressed out.

Then I twigged: she was hungry!

And I was ready. I was so pleased I had the

bottle and milk cartons in my cupboard. I poured the milk into the bottle, and laid her back in my arms – like mums do on the adverts. She choked and spluttered at first, but then she just loved it. She glugged the whole lot down in one go.

I snuggled her up in my arms in the sunshine. She looked woozy, like she was drunk from the milk, and her cheeks were pink, milky and fat. I felt cosy there with her, and sort of daydreamy, like the world was far, far away. Just us two together . . . all wrapped up.

Like in the beach hut.

I shook myself a little. I didn't want to doze off like I had in the hut in case she did another one of her now-you-see-me-now-you-don't specials.

But I felt so sleepy, and my eyelids so heavy . . .

Then out of the corner of an eye, I caught a spark of purple by my window . . . and then another by my door. I wondered if I'd nodded off and was dreaming. More flashes of purple. I opened my eyes wide. It was a tiny, delicate butterfly with pale purple wings. Lavender wings. It fluttered around my room.

I watched it a while, dreamily. A shimmery blur in the sunlight. I closed my eyes and I could still see it. A magic purple sparkle, flashing here and there.

Perhaps it's come from the fairies? Maybe they want Celeste back?

Chapter Eleven

'Please don't take her,' I whispered. 'I promise to look after her. I prom—'

'HIC!'

Celeste shook me from my daze.

'HIC!' She had great big hiccups.

The butterfly flashed purple and flew out of the window.

She started crying and bringing her little legs up and down. She arched her back and squeaked. Did she have tummy ache from the milk? Or maybe she had wind?

'Oh no, Flutterby Baby,' I said. 'Are you full of burp?'

I had an idea you had to pat babies to get burps out: I'd seen a lady do it once on a bus. I laid her over my shoulder and tapped her back with just two fingers – very gently.

No burp.

'Come on,' I said, 'it'll be better out than in.' I got up and held her over my shoulder. I did a dance to jiggle her burp out.

Nothing.

Another gentle pat, and then the burp came . . . along with loads of milk. A whole cow's worth, all over me in a great gush.

Ugh!

It went inside my top and ran down my back, a tickly, warm trickle.

Double ugh.

I put Celeste down and peeled my T-shirt off my back.

I had lumpy milk all in my hair and I stank like an old cheese sarnie. 'Ta a trillion, Stinkerbell!' I said.

Celeste was dead happy though, now she'd got rid of her burps. But she was wet, sicky and cottage-cheesy. We both needed a good bath.

I ran a bath and I stripped us both off. I stepped in carefully, holding her against me. She seemed extra tiny when she was bare. I felt her little back under my fingers, and wished again that she had shimmery fairy wings.

Ever so slowly, I laid her back in the warm water with my palms under her. For a minute, her eyes went wide, and I thought she was going to cry. But then she gazed at the ripply shadows the bath water made on the ceiling, and went into a daze. She liked being a water baby.

Afterwards I wrapped her up in big towel like a baby Jesus in a play. She peeped out with bright eyes and shiny, pink cheeks. She looked brand new.

She's beautiful.

I rubbed her hair dry, so it went soft like dandelion fluff and stuck up in the air.

I got in a big twist, getting myself dressed. It was like after swimming when you have to drag on dry clothes, except even harder because I had to do it one-handed. Celeste wouldn't let me lay her down on the carpet – she just cried like she was hurt. I thought: now she's found me, she's never going to let me put her down ever again. But I didn't mind.

'Shells?'

I jumped. It was Mum and she was right outside the door.

'What you doing in there, babe? I really need the loo.'

Chapter Twelve

'OK, give me a tick.'

I whisked Mum's big, pink dressing gown off the back of the door and bundled Celeste up in it, with just her nose peeping out for air.

I unlocked the door.

Mum was stood there, shivering in one of Toadstool's big, honky T-shirts instead of a proper nightie. She looked like her body was awake, but not her face. And she looked so little, even more than usual.

'C'mon!' she said. 'I need a pee. Who you

chatting on to?'

Oh no, she'd heard me talking to Celeste.

'I was playing a kind of game,' I muttered, not looking at her.

She yawned. 'Yeah well, let me in there now.'

'Yes, Mu—'

'HIC!'

I leapt in the air.

'HIC!' I jumped again. Celeste was hiccuping inside the dressing gown. How could she still have wind after all that sick?

'What you doing?' said Mum.

'HIC!'

'Oh, I got hiccups . . .' I said. 'Pardon me!'

'HIC!' went Celeste again. I couldn't help but giggle.

Mum looked at me, confused. She had old mascara smudged over one of her cheeks.

'Stop faffing around, Shell – I'm actually bursting!' she snapped. Then, more gently: 'Sorry, chick. Got a bit of a headache still, see.'

Yeah, because of all the pink wine you downed.

I moved out of her way and started towards my

room when I felt warmness spreading over my top. And wetness. Oh no, Celeste didn't have a nappy on, and she must have done a wee on me.

'Oh, and Shells,' said Mum, 'what you doing with my dressing gown? Give us it, please. It's freezing.'

'No . . .' I said quickly.

Mum stared at me.

'Uh?'

'I mean, you can't have it because I . . . er . . . did a wee on it.' As soon as I said it I knew it was the dumbest thing to have said – ever.

Mum wrinkled her nose.

'You did a WEE on my dressing gown,' she said, her voice all high with not believing her ears. She shook her head slowly. 'Don't be flipping daft, Shells, of course you didn't.'

Before I could move out of the way, Mum reached for the dressing gown and pulled it. I felt Celeste start to slide and fall inside the bundle.

'NO!' I yelled.

I grabbed at the air, but I couldn't feel her. My eyes flew across the floor, but she was nowhere.

Mum was holding the dressing gown.

It was empty.

Celeste was gone. Vanished into thin air.

And Mum was looking at me like I was a bonkers child.

'Shelley . . . what's going on? Are you all right?'

'Yes,' I said, quickly. 'Just mucking around. Playing . . .'

She wouldn't normally have believed that. She'd have quizzed me more. But she just sighed and rubbed her eyes. I thought she was going to say something, but she just patted my arm weakly, put on the dressing gown and shuffled into the bathroom.

I stood there in the hallway, chewing my wet hair. Everything had gone horrible again. Celeste had disappeared off to Fairyland – without even a nappy on. Mum was even more mooey, and now wearing a dressing gown covered in baby fairy wee.

And I was alone. Again.

Then I heard a squeak from my room. My favourite kind.

Chapter Thirteen

And there she was on my bed. Happy as a chocolate bunny, cooing away to herself.

But how had she blinking well managed that?

Well, I had to give it to her – she had cool, baby-fairy style, getting away from Mum like that. I wished I could just fly away whenever I felt like it.

'But hang on . . .' My mind started catching up. She'd been all damp and bare-bummed inside that towel when she'd disappeared, and now she was dressed again. I unpopped her suit, and she had a clean nappy on too.

'How did you do that, dumpling?' I whispered. 'How did you get those clothes back on again? And where'd that nappy come from? Did you fly off and find your nice mummy?'

Lucky you.

I nuzzled her fuzzy head and stroked her softly. 'Where do you come from, eh? I know I'm not just making you up, because you're as real as me. But I just don't get it . . .'

I wondered if anyone else had ever had a flying, magic baby to babysit. Anyone who wasn't in a storybook or a total nut job. I wanted to ask someone, but who could I ask? Definitely not Mum . . . she couldn't even cope with going to the loo at the moment.

I wondered what would happen if I Googled 'magic baby'. I knew Toadstool had left his laptop here, but obviously I wasn't allowed to use it and he kept his dumb password a secret.

'Shells?'

I jumped. Mum was calling through my door. 'Could you go and buy some loo roll, sweetheart?

We're right out.'

'OK, Mum.'

'There's my good girl, ta. There's some coins in my purse.'

Not as many now . . .

But, oh no, what was I saying? I couldn't go to the Co-op again! I was probably barred . . . No, I would have to go the little corner shop by the library.

The library . . .

Ah, sharp idea! I could use the old library computers while I was over there, couldn't I? Look up baby magicness. Or maybe even find a book.

But how stupid was I going to sound?

'Hello, Mrs Nice Librarian Lady, I'd like a book called *A Crazy Girl's Guide to Invisible Babies* please. Ta, lovely.'

Still, it was worth a try. Of course Celeste had to come too.

'Promise to be a good girl at the boring library, angel face?' I said, kissing her.

Celeste looked at me like she was listening hard.

Then she went pink in the face, and made a great big whiff. A dirty nappy.

'Cheeky monkey.' I laughed. 'That's not very angel-ish, is it?'

It took me ages to get her ready after that – loads of wiping and changing and feeding and faffing about.

And it was peeing down again. I found a waterproof in the landing wardrobe. It was Toadstool's old one, and it was huge and mushroomy and *vile*, but just perfect: it zipped right around me and Celeste like a poncho. I kept my arms inside so I could hold her against me, and put the hood up so no one would know it was me.

I sneaked past Mum's room. I could see her through the crack of the door again – she was talking on the phone.

I stopped on the landing to earwig.

'Please ring me back, Scotty.' Her voice was all cracked. 'I know you're getting my messages. Just talk to me, eh? I need you . . . I'm in a mess without you . . .'

She so is . . .

But I don't want him to come back . . .

My throat went all swallowy like I might cry too, so I hurried down the stairs, and out to the back gate. I waddled off down the quiet back lane – because there was no way I was going out the front looking fat and loopy like that.

I was getting a bit warm with Celeste inside the coat, but it was nice to feel her cuddled up against me. She found her thumb, and slowly settled down in her little tent before kipping out, sparko.

Then I stopped dead.

There was a yellow and black stripy bike leant against a gate.

The Wasp Bike!

Yes, it was definitely the same bike that Chicken Boy had been riding. Chicken Boy – Slugface's new little mate. And it was outside a house with a big 'SOLD' sign. Slugface had said Chicken Boy had just moved to town.

Uh-oh.

Chapter Fourteen

I whirled round, but I couldn't see any boys anywhere.

I heard a scuffly noise coming from a garden.

And another scuffle. And a little dog stuck his nose through the gate, wagging and wagging his tail. I reckoned he was a poodle puppy, but not a posh, pompommy one: he had a hairdo like a little lamb. He was the colour of chocolate buttons, and had big, melty eyes. He was so super cute I wanted to stuff him in my coat-tent with Celeste and take him home with me.

'Winns!' A man's voice came from the house. Chicken Boy's dad? I crouched lower behind the hedge. 'Winnie! Get here!' The little dog trotted off, still wagging.

Winnie? Like 'Winnie the Pooh'? Then I giggled to myself. Of course! He was a poodle dog, so he was called Winnie the Poo-dle. Bit soppy, but cute. I was dying to know if I was right and they really did call him that.

But I had to go in case Chicken Boy came out for his bike. With his Slugface mate. I walked away really fast, glancing behind me all the time as I went.

Celeste was still asleep when we got to the library. I kept her inside my dripping coat and just put my hood down.

The duff old computers were all being used, so I made my way to the children's section. But I couldn't see any fairy books there, except dopey picture books for toddlers. I waddled to the adult shelves where I spotted one book called *Fairies*, but spelt in a wonky old-fashioned way, like *Faeries*. That was more like it.

I went and found a quiet corner and flicked through the fairy pages. I was secretly hoping to find a bit that said: '*If an invisible baby suddenly magics itself onto your bed, then you know you're babysitting a real-life baby fairy . . . and you can wish for anything you like.*'

Of course it didn't say that anywhere. Shame . . .

But it *did* say only the Victorians thought fairies were small and fluttery, and in fact fairies could be as big as human children and wingless.

Like Celeste.

And even better, on another page it said that nearly *everyone* believed in fairies in the olden days, and once two little girls even took photos of some. I went all tingly when I read that. See, I wasn't so mad then, was I?

I flicked to another bit:

'*Adults often view children's fairy sightings as mere childish games with "imaginary friends" – or as a symptom of disturbance or stress.*'

Imaginary friends? Would Mum think that if I told her about Celeste? Huh! There was no way she was imaginary – because that meant see-through, and not really there. Celeste was magic, but she was real, all right.

Still, I didn't much like the word 'disturbance'. Didn't that mean being as crazy as a lollipop? And I wasn't that stressed . . .

Was I?

The book wasn't helping at all. I stuffed it back on a shelf . . . stupid book, stupid library. And I was getting completely boiling in the coat too. Time to go.

The rain had stopped. Celeste was waking up – moaning in her sleep, wriggling and huffling. She felt damp, so I unzipped the coat just a little.

Celeste looked shocked at the open air. She blinked her big eyes at the light and squeaked – like she'd just been born again.

'Yeah, it's a big, bad world out here, baby girl,' I whispered into her soft head. 'We just need to buy some bog roll, and then we'll go home.'

I hurried through the puddles to the corner shop.

Mistake.

Chapter Fifteen

I was at the till paying for the bog roll and some cheeky toffees – and trying to look normal in my massive coat with a wiggly Celeste-lump inside – when I felt a sniff-snuffling at my feet.

Winnie the Poodle. On a lead.

Oh no!

I swung round.

On the other end of Winnie's lead was Chicken Boy.

He recognised me and a big grin spread across his face. It was odd because at first I thought it was an actual, proper friendly grin. But then he ruined it . . .

'Oh, hi, Belle!'

What the . . . ! There he goes again. Copying Slugface's mean jelly-belly names . . .

I felt my face go red. He was the last person I wanted to see, looking all fat in my coat-tent holding a huge bag of sweets.

I pushed past him. Celeste grumbled in her sleep

'My name's Shelley, actually!' I snapped. The words kind of popped out without me meaning them to.

'Oh . . . sorry!' His eyes went wide. 'I didn't realise. I thought . . .' And he seemed to go red too.

Like he really is sorry. Like he really hadn't realised.

I opened my mouth to say it was OK. But just then Celeste kicked her legs into my tummy so an 'ooof' came out instead.

Jay looked surprised. 'Sorry? What?'

I can't talk to him, not with Celeste here. He's going to think I'm a loon.

'Nothing, I just . . .' But then over his shoulder,

out of the shop window, I saw a disgusting sight.

Slugface.

Riding past on a bike that was too small for him. He seemed to be looking for someone. And – hang on – that was the Wasp Bike he was on! Chicken Boy must have lent him it.

Yuck. What am I doing talking to one of Slugface's friends? It's probably a trap.

Without another word, I made for the door, checking that Slugface had gone before I opened it.

Winnie was yapping behind me. And then he legged it out the door and across the road, with his lead dragging behind him.

'Winnie!' Jay bolted past and after Winnie, who'd raced into someone's garden.

In the distance I could see Slugface coming back our way on the Wasp bike.

Oh no, this is too blinking much!

Celeste was too heavy for me to run. But I decided I didn't want to die yet, so I ducked inside the little kiddies' park next to the shop, and nipped down behind a low-hanging bush by the brambly back wall.

Just in time.

'Winns, where are you? Get here!'

I sneaked a quick look and spied someone by the baby swings. Someone with red chicken-ish hair.

Oh, why can't he just bog off?!

'Winnie! Where've you gone? . . .' Chicken Boy sounded well miffed.

I pulled my elbows and knees in tight so no bits of me were sticking out. Suddenly I felt a sneeze coming, but I held my nose until it went away. Celeste was scrunched up against my tummy. She was still crying – not really properly, just little worried yelps like a kitten miaowing. She didn't like our hide-and-seek game one bit.

I could still hear Chicken Boy calling, but more distant. His voice was all high – like ladies use to call their cats at night.

'Winneeeeeee!' he sang

I giggled to myself, and sang the Winnie-the-Pooh song to Celeste under my breath. She looked at me, surprised, her eyes wide and brimming with tears. 'I expect they've got a cat called Tigger and a guinea-Piglet too!' I whispered.

Celeste stopped bleating, and found her thumb. Slowly I started to relax too. It was nice in that corner, hidden away – just me and her. The sun came out, making the wet grass steam gently. I pulled off our coat-tent so we could sunbathe a bit. A fat bee buzzed around in the tangle of daisies and buttercups, and the air smelt of sweet, ripe blackberries.

I loved this park. Even though it was ages ago when I was still in Reception, I could remember Mum bringing me there.

She'd push me on the swings and play about on the roundabout. Sometimes we even brought a picnic. We used to come a lot . . . but then when she met Toadstool, she'd never have time to stop long after school. She'd always have to get back for him – to cook his tea and that.

Manky Toadstool the big ruiner.

I pushed the thought of him away, and thought of me and Mum again . . .

Something tickled my ear and flapped tiny wings in my face. A little butterfly with lavender wings. Another one! It was just like the one in the house the other day.

The butterfly landed on Celeste's fluffy hair, which was shining in the sunlight like a golden halo.

'Look at you,' I said. 'You look like a baby angel. Is that what you are? Or maybe you're even more important than an angel – like a girl Jesus. That would be cool.'

I was feeling dozy in the warm sunshine. I had that lovely, woozy feeling again, all wrapped up with her, safe and snug. Like we were blurred together.

Celeste kipped out, breathing soft little breaths. Her eyelids fluttered like the butterfly's wings. Dandelion fluff floated around us, silvery in the sunlight like fairy dust.

'Win! Winnneeee!'

I jolted upright. I'd almost forgotten about Chicken Boy. His voice was nearer now.

'Winneee!'

And nearer . . .

A small, wet nose appeared behind the bush,

followed by chocolate curls, a waggy tail and a dragging lead.

Winnie. Oh no!

'Shoo . . . pssst!' I hissed. But he wagged harder and gave a short, yappy bark.

He came right up to sleepyhead Celeste and seemed to sniff her. He wagged even harder.

Can he see Celeste?

'Push off!' I shoved him away, but he thought that was the best game ever and wagged his whole body as well as his tail.

'Winnie! For God's sake . . .' Chicken Boy sounded cross now.

And much closer.

He was going to find me any minute.

Chapter Sixteen

Suddenly I had a brainwave. I picked up a small stone and showed it to Winnie.

'Look . . . good boy, fetch!' I whispered, and rolled it gently away from me. Winnie leapt after it, nearly doing a double-triple somersault in his rush, yapping his woolly head off. I peeped out of our leafy den, and saw him grab the stone, run across the playground and out the gate.

'There you are!' said Chicken Boy. The wet grass squeaked under his trainers as he sprinted after him. I breathed a big sigh of relief. But then there was a screech of bike brakes from the street. And footsteps. Coming back towards me. And then Chicken Boy dived behind our bush, nearly squashing us flat. He looked shock-horrified to see me, but he stayed where he was.

'Oi, Jay!' came a voice. It was Slugface! Chicken Boy looked at me. He shook his head and put his finger to his lips. SSHHHH!

Chicken Boy is hiding from his new bezzie mate?

'Where are you, Jay-jay, you big girlie-wuss?' jeered Slugface. 'Come and get your baby tricycle!'

Oh dear – perhaps not so bezzie-matey after all.

Of course our hiding place was rubbish. So in about one and a half seconds Slugface's fat head appeared behind the tree. He roared with delight when he saw us both there. He threw the Wasp Bike down into some nettles and grabbed us both by the wrists. He was so strong I didn't have a chance of wriggling free. I nearly dropped Celeste, who started crying.

'Hiding from me?' he hissed in Chicken Boy's face.

Then he twisted my wrist so tightly it burnt. 'And I want a word with you, fat Belly . . . about the other day,' he spat.

He swung us together roughly. 'Kissy kissy,' he said.

I held on tight to Celeste and stuck out my elbows to stop her from being crushed between us. Chicken Boy's head smashed into mine. A sharp pain cut across my eyes.

Celeste howled.

And grew . . . into a great big toddler again, just like that.

She clung round my waist with her baby footballer thighs and squawked with rage at Slugface, her face beetroot and streaming with tears.

Chicken Boy fell back on the grass, holding his forehead. I wondered if he was properly hurt.

I looked at Slugface's big, laughing ugly mug. I heard Celeste's screaming in my ears, in my head. Heat crept up my neck and into my face, and then I just flipped. I heard myself bellow along with Celeste.

'GET LOST!' I ran and shoved Slugface hard in his chest. Really hard.

I took him by surprise. Or maybe it was the weight of me and Celeste together. He fell down, flat on his back, with a thud.

I toppled and fell backwards too. Celeste landed on me, winding me. She was panting and red. She rolled off me and threw herself face down on the ground, screeching and tearing up tiny fistfuls of grass.

It was some tantrum.

I sat there stupidly – feeling faint.

What is happening to me, fighting with Slugface? I'm normally so quiet and scaredy.

Then with a sharp yap, Winnie came bounding out of nowhere.

Slugface was still lying like a big splat on the grass, swearing. I'd knocked all the puff out of him. Winnie ran and stood over him, barking so hard his paws nearly lifted off the ground.

Slugface whimpered, and tried to wriggle away.

'Get that stupid, fluffy slipper away from me or I'll kick its teeth in,' he stammered.

Winnie put his front paws on Slugface's tummy and yapped right in his ear. Slugface squealed and curled into a ball.

Oh.

My.

God.

Big, ugly Slugface was scared of tiny, fluffy Winnie!

Chicken Boy was suddenly at my side. He pointed at Slugface and Winnie, made a face, and we both laughed. He offered me his hand and pulled me up, grinning.

I grinned back at him, and at the exact moment our eyes met, I felt Celeste vanish . . .

I looked around at the spot where she'd been having her red-out on the grass. She'd definitely gone – just like that, *poof*!

Whoa, what happened there?

I had no time to think. 'Watch this!' said Chicken Boy, nudging me. 'See him off, Winnie,' he called out. 'ROBBERS!'

That one word made Winnie do his nut with barking.

Slugface yelped. 'Get him off me!'

'No way! Bite him, Winnie,' said Chicken Boy.

'ROBBERS!' Winnie's yapping revved up and up.

'Oh dear, poor Brandon. He's being bullied by a slipper,' I said.

Chicken Boy laughed. 'Little tiny poodles make you cack your pants?' he called to Slugface, over the noise. 'Well, you'd better leave us alone now, you big marshmallow, or we're going to tell every kid in town about this. And if they don't believe us then we'll bring Winnie to find you, and they can watch you run away like a piglet. OK?'

'Yes, yes . . . just call him off!' Slugface was practically begging.

'It's a promise, then? You'll leave us alone?'

Slugface nodded.

'All right, see you later then, Pet Shop Boy,' said Chicken Boy. 'You're safe now – I'm taking the scary poodle away.'

He swung Winnie up into his arms, and we went out of the playground together, shrieking with laughter.

I hooked my shopping bag out of the bush as

I went past, glancing around for Celeste – just in case – but somehow I just knew she wouldn't be there. And I didn't have time to miss her – not with Jay gabbling on to me.

Chapter Seventeen

'That boy is such a doof,' said Chicken Boy. I was carrying a wriggling Winnie while he pushed his Wasp Bike along the pavement. I wasn't sure where we were heading, but I wanted to chat.

'He's a *total* creep! Slugface – that's my pet name for him,' I said. 'But I thought you were friends!'

'No way! I was only hanging around with him that first day because I didn't know any other kids,' he said. 'We've only just moved here from Brighton. Brandon was in the park by himself, and he just started following me about.'

'He always does that with new people,' I said. 'Until they find out what a loser he is.'

I could even feel sorry for him if he wasn't such a pile of mould.

'Yeah, and then when I didn't want to go round with him every day, he turned all psycho and hunted me.'

'He's a bit messed up. You got to keep away from him,' I said.

We were at the top of Jay's street. He stopped and looked at me shyly.

'Hey, and sorry about the Belly-Belle thing. I'm stupid – I should have guessed it was just Brandon being a sicko. But Belle *is* actually a real name, so . . .' He shrugged.

'It's fine.' I smiled.

'Nah, but you were NOT happy.' He laughed. 'And seeing how you flew at Brandon, I wouldn't want to be on the wrong end of you.'

I laughed too.

'It's taken me since I was five to stand up to him. I don't really know what happened to me.'

Celeste started it, the stroppy madam!

'Well, go you,' Jay said. 'Girl power. He so had it coming.'

Yeah, and it'd felt good getting cross . . .

'Look, do you want to come to mine for a bit?' he said. 'My dad's out at work, so we could scoff stuff and watch telly.'

'OK . . .'

This is a bit odd. Chicken Boy wants to be friends with me.

'And by the way, Brandon got my name wrong too. It isn't Jay-jay girlie-wuss. It's actually Jade Whiteson.'

I stopped.

'Jade?' I spluttered.

'Yeah. But everyone just calls me "Jay".'

WHAT? Chicken Boy is a girl!

Chicken Girl.

'Oh God!' I said. 'I thought –'

'– that I was a boy?' She laughed.

'Well, um,' I blithered, 'it's not that you look like a boy, it's just –'

'– my short hair, boys' clothes, boys' bike. I know. Don't worry – I don't care.' She beamed at me. It was a nice smile. She definitely looked a lot like a girl when she smiled like that. And nothing like a chicken.

We went up his – *her* – path and into the house. There were packing boxes everywhere.

I thought of the girls' bracelet I'd seen on her wrist. It made sense now.

'That was a giveaway though, your bracelet.' I pointed to it. 'It's a bit girlie.'

'Friendship bracelet, present from my cousin,' she said matter-of-factly. 'I like her so I wear it – but it's not my thing really. I think it looks a bit silly.' She stopped on her doorstep and looked at me hard. 'And talking of looking silly . . . do you know you've got a lump of bubblegum stuck in your hair?'

I'd completely forgotten. How woolly-brained could I be? So while Jay got busy making toast, I went upstairs to their bathroom to de-gum myself.

The gum was completely matted in. Mum was going to fuss if it wouldn't come out . . . well, that's if she stopped crying long enough to look at me.

My breath caught in my throat.

Suddenly I just wanted Celeste again.

But then Jay called up to me:

'Toast's ready!'

'Coming! Gimme half a tick.' I gave up trying to pull the gum out – I'd had enough of moping in the bathroom by myself. So I took their nail scissors and cut off a big, gummy chunk of my fringe.

I looked at myself in the mirror.

I looked like a chewed chimp.

The kids were really going to bash me at my new stupid school looking like that. *Just blinking perfect . . .*

But the sight of Jay with a tray piled with toast and big mugs of hot chocolate cheered me up no end. And she never said a word about my chimp hairdo. We sat munching away happily together, chatting on. We watched some telly and then a film.

Soon the afternoon was whizzing by – and it was so fun that I mostly forgot to worry about Mum and Celeste. Apart from sending Mum a quick text to say I'd be back in a bit with the loo roll.

Just in case she cared.

Jay got out her laptop and we were just mucking about on it when I spied a board game on top of a packing box.

'Oh, I know that game,' I said. It was called *One for the Pot*. 'I used to love it!' I remembered playing it at school-holiday club.

'Yeah – I loved it too! I made Dad keep it,' said Jay. 'Wanna play?'

It was a dappy game. We both knew it was too young for us, but we didn't care.

She filled up the plastic teapot with water, and then we each had our own teacup. The idea was that if you landed on certain squares you had to get some pours of water, or a spoon or some plastic sugar lumps in your cup. The cups filled up fast, and the winner was the one whose cup overflowed last.

At first we played it sensibly. Taking it in turns, and not cheating. But not for long.

'You need to do bigger pours than that!' said Jay. 'Like this.' She grabbed the teapot, and sloshed water into my cup and onto my jeans.

'Well, I think you need some more sugar lumps in yours – make you sweeter,' I said. I threw all the plastic sugar lumps into her cup, making a small tidal wave of water flop over the side onto her lap.

By the end we were tipping whole teapotfuls down each other's necks, and giggling like idiots. It was a full-on water fight. I decided I liked Jay way more now she wasn't Chicken Boy. She was definitely better as my friend than my enemy.

My friend . . .

I had a sudden thought:

'Hey, what school you going to in September?' I asked, wringing out my T-shirt.

'Wirthing,' she said.

'Me too!'

We grinned at each other.

Maybe I'll have someone to go around with after all . . .

Jay was just refilling the teapot from the bathroom tap when the door banged downstairs

'That'll be my dad back,' she said.

'Oh no, will he be cross?' I said, looking at the

wet everywhere. Toadstool would have barbecued me alive.

'Nah, Dad's cool about stuff,' she said.

'And what about your mum?'

'Oh, my mum died when I was born.' She said it just like that. As if it was nothing much.

'God, sorry,' I said.

'Yeah, well, it's fine.' Jay shrugged. 'I got my dad.'

I nodded. 'I haven't got a dad . . . my mum was only sixteen when she had me, and he was just some boy. I've never even met him.' I shrugged too. 'So I've only ever had my mum. And then later a sort-of stepdad too, worse luck.'

Who's hopefully GONE now . . .

There was a soft knock at the door.

A bald head with glasses popped round. 'Hey, Jay. You entertaining?'

'Yeah, Dad, this is my new friend Shelley.'

'Hi, Shelley.' He smiled at me. And then he made a thinking face. 'Hang on, I know you . . .'

My brain caught up too.

He was the Nice Manager Man from the Co-op.

My heart started galloping.

Oh no! First I mess up your shop. And now I've watered your house . . .

Maybe Jay was wrong and he was going to tell me off.

But what he said was even worse.

'Yeah, you were in yesterday buying nappies, weren't you?'

'Oh, your mum's got a baby?' said Jay. 'How old?'

'Um . . . small,' I said. I couldn't exactly say she didn't have one, could I?

I felt my face was on fire – I knew I'd gone red.

I can't be Jay's friend now. Because then she'll find out I'm lying.

'Yeah – der! Babies usually *are* small.' She gave me a funny look. 'Hey, what's up? You've gone kind of cross-eyed.'

'I'm fine,' I said. 'Got to get back actually, sorry. Look, it's nearly six already. But ta for the toast. And bye, Mr . . . er . . . Jay's dad.'

I scurried out of their house and away down the road, still burning up.

Chapter Eighteen

They lived three doors up from the pub. So I'd only gone about ten steps when I heard a laugh coming from the open window of the bar.

Oh no.

I knew that laugh. Kind of squeaky and fake.

It was Mum's pretend laugh. The one she kept specially for Toadstool's bad jokes.

Toadstool. One big bad joke on legs.

I crept up to the open window just as a man spoke. Yep, it was Toadstool's creepy croak.

Mum had found him.

Ugh, no.

And it was him for sure because I could see his duff old van in the pub car park – the one he used for his sort of job, moving stuff about for people. Not that he worked much. It was way easier to scav off Mum. She was always buying his fags and beer.

I crouched down under the open window.

Cars kept going past, so it was hard to catch every word, but I knew Mum wasn't laughing any more. I could tell by her voice she was getting upset.

I strained to hear.

'I miss you . . .'

' . . . where've you been?'

'Please let's talk about it . . .'

She's practically begging. Yuck!

Toadstool grunted something, but two motorbikes went by so I missed it.

'OK, but let me come away with you,' Mum replied.

What?

I tried to get hold of her words. I screwed up my face.

Let me come away with you . . . My tummy flipped – and double back-flipped again.

Where's Mum going? Is she leaving me behind?

I stood up too quickly and whacked my head on the open window.

'Owww!' I couldn't help squealing.

Toadstool was at the window in a second.

'Shelley!' He looked at me like I was some dog poo. 'What the hell's she doing here, creeping around listening?' he bellowed. 'For Christ's sake, Trina, that girl does my flipping nut! There's never a minute's peace . . .'

Mum appeared at the window then too. She was all dolled up again.

She looked at me with a face like a frightened rabbit, and then turned back inside.

'No, Scott, I'm sure she wasn't listening . . .'

I heard him swear. Really bad words.

He's not pretending to be all nicey-nicey about me any more, is he? Perhaps now Mum'll see what he really thinks of me.

But no . . .

'Scotty, you don't mean that . . .' she pleaded.

She isn't going to stand up to him, is she . . .
As per usual.

Their voices trailed off.

Oh no, I hope they're not coming out here . . .

I just ran. My heart was booming, and I couldn't remember how to breathe. I just wanted to get home and hide under my bed.

Chapter Nineteen

I slammed the front door hard behind me, and leant against it, panting. My head was whirling, and I felt a bit sick.

My eyes were filling. Again.

Where is Mum going away to? Without me?

And why can't she SEE what Toadstool's like?

I took a deep breath to make my crying go away, but instead a big wail came out of my mouth.

Straight after I heard a noise.

Inside the house.

Upstairs?

Sniffing, I wiped my eyes and listened. For a minute I was scared that Toadstool had somehow beaten me back, and James-Bonded himself in through the upstairs window. Just so he could shout at me . . .

More noise. Crying.

Then I got it . . .

Celeste. Of course!

I bolted up the stairs.

She was on my bed, just like the day she'd first come. Tiny, weeny newborn again. And crying her little heart out.

I rushed to her and held her to me.

'I know how you feel, baby girl,' I whispered. I felt tears plop off my nose again.

I rocked her for ages, softly singing and singing. I kept having to wipe our faces. At least an hour must have passed, but Mum wasn't home yet.

Mum . . .

Has she just gone away and left me? With not even a goodbye?

Without bothering to get into my nightie, I put

us to bed, and we snuggled up together. But I kept on sneezing, which made Celeste jump.

I hoped I wasn't getting poorly.

Would Mum even look after me now she's like this?

I pulled my duvet right over our heads. We sucked our thumbs and I twirled our hair.

I want to hide like this forever . . . just me and Celeste . . .

Next thing I knew someone was shaking me gently.

My room was light again. I could tell it was early morning.

'Celeste?' I said, feeling around for her without opening my eyes properly.

She was gone.

More shaking.

'Darling, it's me,' came a whisper.

My eyes flicked open.

Mum!

'It's OK – don't panic. I just need to talk to you.' She was sat on my bed. She looked flushed and excited. Her hair was wet, and she was already dressed and made up all pretty.

I sat up.

'What . . . are you going with Scott now?'

She touched my cheek. She smelled really flowery. Too much perfume.

'Ahh, so you *did* hear what Scott said at the pub?'

I just stopped myself from making a face when she said his name.

I hung my head and nodded.

Was she going to be cross with me for earwigging?

But she just carried on, talking fast.

'Yes, I am going, babe – but I have to, see. Please understand. It's a chance to try and sort things out. He's got to collect a van-load from Birmingham today and he said I can go with him. That way we'll get a bit of time together, to talk alone, without . . .' She stopped herself, but I knew what she meant. Without being interrupted.

By me.

'OK,' I said, pretending to stretch and avoiding her eyes.

What about me, Mum?

'We're going to stay in a motel on the way back tonight – my treat – and . . .' now Mum looked down away and blushed, '. . . and Trace said you can have her sofa. I already texted her.'

Trace was Mum's friend from two roads up. She had a tiny house, three kids, and a rough mouth on her. Mum didn't even like her that much. There was no way I was going there.

Mum saw my face and went redder.

'OK, sorry, not Trace's then . . . but who else?' She was begging me with her eyes.

'It's all right, don't worry, Mum,' I said, quickly. 'I'll go to Lexi's.' I missed out the part about Lexi being in Ibiza.

She squeezed my hand. 'That's my good girl. And don't worry – it'll all be OK again soon. He'll see sense.'

OK again. With Toadstool back here?

I didn't want Mum to be sad. But I didn't want to see Toadstool ever again. Both ways were horrible.

My hands balled into fists under the duvet.

I pressed my lips together to stop any crying coming, and I had this huge frog in my throat.

Mum even didn't notice. Her eyes just kept flitting to her watch.

'I thought he'd be here by now, actually,' she muttered, twisting her hands. 'But I said he couldn't have his stuff back unless he let me come. So he has to show up, doesn't he!'

The doorbell went.

'Oh, phew,' said Mum, jumping up, flustered. 'That'll be him.' She fluffed up her hair and straightened her dress.

She kissed my head.

'Bye darling,' she said. Then she paused for a moment and looked at me, her eyes like the old Mum. 'So you'll be all right at Lexi's for a couple of days, eh?'

'Course,' I said, brightly.

She sort of stroked the duvet, and then tritt-trotted across my room – she was wearing stupidly high shoes.

'Oh, and Shells . . .' She turned back at the door. 'I just pulled everything out of the hall cupboard looking for my going-away bag. It's a bit of a mess. Do you think you could put it all away for me before you go? I got to rush now . . .'

'Yes, Mum.' I pretended to yawn. All casual.

'Thanks, doll. Love ya!'

I heard her trit her way down the stairs. The door slammed. And she was gone.

Gone.

I shivered even though I was wrapped in my covers.

The house felt so quiet. All I could hear were the nasty gulls.

How could she leave me?

Alone.

She'd never left me by myself overnight before. OK, she thought I was going to Lexi's, but the old Mum would've rung and double-checked with Lexi's parents. The old Mum would have fussed about it.

Not now . . . her head's way too full of Scott.

I screwed my face up and tried to go back to sleep, but I couldn't just lie there. I felt like I had prickles running all over me, and my chest hurt.

I leapt up and stomped around my room – up and down, up and down, like I was trying to get away from something that was chasing me. My chest ached so much now I thought I might stop breathing.

Celeste . . . Mum . . . Celeste . . .

I trampled through all the stuff on my floor. Still walking . . . kicking things harder for no reason until I stubbed my toe on my bed.

It really hurt.

That did it.

Without thinking, I picked up a book and threw it at the wall.

There was a massive crash. Much louder than a book on a wall makes.

Coming from downstairs.

This time I knew what it was.

Celeste.

I took the stairs in a few bounds.

The hall looked like a junk yard where Mum had dragged heaps of stuff out of the cupboard to get to her bag, and left it all over the floor. I ignored it.

Celeste was there, all right.

Sat on the kitchen floor, having a full-on red-out. Bawling her little head off in a roaring rage, her face crumpled and pink.

And she was surrounded by every kitchen-ish thing we owned. Tupperware, saucepans, sugar, tins of beans, pegs and pots, split, empty packets – everywhere. It looked like we'd had robbers in.

And why was she brown and smeary? In fact, everything looked brown and smeary. The lino was speckled with brown polka dots. Chocolate buttons. Melted everywhere.

The kitchen had already been a mess, but this was something else.

I stood there open-mouthed, and watched while she pulled herself up onto her feet using a table leg, and stood there wobbling.

Her face was running with tears. I touched my cheek and realised how much I was crying too.

'WAAAAAA!' She tugged fiercely at a tea towel on the table. My door keys and two mugs smashed onto the floor. She flumped back down on her nappy bottom with a sharp squeal, and threw herself backwards in temper onto the lino, kicking her legs, banging her head and sobbing.

'Mamamama!' she screamed. 'Mama!'

Whoa, some tantrum! Proper drama-queen style.

Her fingers fell on my keys, and she lobbed them away from her as if it was all their fault. They disappeared down behind the radiator.

I started out of my daze and stepped forward to try and hook the keys out, my feet crunching on a carpet of Rice Krispies. But I couldn't reach them.

Great . . .

I felt heat rush over me again. And more tears trickled from my eyes.

No key . . . and I couldn't even ask Mum to help.

Because she'd gone.

I kicked up the Rice Krispies into a snowstorm. I booted a bean tin against the wall. On purpose.

I hate Mum!

'I hate her,' I said out loud. 'I HATE HER!' I yelled.

Celeste roared too. Like she was joining in. Egging me on.

She grabbed a ripped packet of pasta, and flung it in the air.

'MAMAMA!' she yelled, and blew a big raspberry.

I was fuming, but somehow that got me laughing. It was like a switch. Then I just couldn't stop. I was hysterical.

'Yeah!' I shrieked. 'Great, big, fat raspberries to Mama.' I sank down on the floor next to her and laughed and laughed and laughed. Celeste's face was still teary, but she started giggling too and upended a bag of noodles next to a small hill of sugar. She grinned at me, naughtily.

'Yes, what a bad, mad mess you've made!' I said to her. 'Well, good. I'm not cleaning it up. Mum can. And bog-breath Toadstool!'

I snatched a bottle of Mum's diet lemonade from the side and shook it hard. I twisted the lid open and lemonade exploded out everywhere. I showered the kitchen with froth.

Celeste shrieked with delight.

'Yahooooo!' I yelled. I took up a big packet of cornflakes and threw golden handfuls into the air. I lobbed two iced buns at the window. Toadstool's fat-boy food. One stuck to the glass like a doughy slug.

Celeste was digging her sharp little nails into me, and trying to mountaineer up my legs. I picked her up, and we danced and whirled and slid up and down on the lino, crashing into all the junk on the floor. My socks bunched up under my feet and I kept nearly falling over. We laughed and laughed like loons.

My socks were getting wet. The floor was slimy under the Rice Krispies. Eggs! Celeste had been in the fridge too . . . what a good idea. I took out one of Mum's yoghurts . . .

'Let's make it slidier,' I said, tipping the yoghurt all over the lino. It worked a total treat – we skidded much faster.

'This is soooo much fun!' I felt wild with badness.

I made cream cheese snowballs and threw them at the ceiling. Celeste laughed and laughed. Then

I filled Toadstool's rank trainers with ham and chutney, swung them by their laces and let them fly.

I took a swig of apple juice straight from the carton – Mum hates it when I do that. I filled my mouth with juice and then squashed my cheeks hard with my hands. The juice squirted across the kitchen – it went miles . . . It was such a cool game – kind of like face water-pistols. Celeste wanted a go too. Soon we were both soaking and giggling and sitting in puddles.

Stuck to the fridge was a faded, cheapo Valentine's card that Toadstool had sent Mum once – probably only so he could get some cash out of her.

'Squirt this way, Celeste,' I said, pointing at the crummy card.

We used it for target practice until it was hanging and soggy, and all the juice had gone.

'Expect Mum will still keep that card though. She'll probably frame it, won't she?' I told Celeste.

Celeste put some noodles on her head like pretend hair.

'Ooh, look at you, Goldilocks,' I said. 'Pretty.'

'Pwetty,' she said. 'Pwetty 'Ell.'

'No, you're not called Shell, you dollop, *I'm* Shell,' I said to her. 'I know – let's have some make-up to go with your pwetty noodle hairdo.' I melted some chocolate buttons in my hand and made her chocolate blusher, lipstick and eyeshadow. She stayed really still and let me do it, peering up at me with her big lavender eyes.

'There you go. Now you really do look like a bad fairy – a little chocolate goblin.' I stuck some Rice Krispies on the thick chocolate on her cheeks. 'And these are your warts.' I made up my own face too – and gave us both a chocolate star tattoo on our arms. I tried giving us fake tan with peanut butter, but it was the crunchy kind so it was too scratchy.

Celeste found a jam doughnut in a bag. She squeezed it so hard the jam oozed out everywhere. She blobbed some on the wall. Jam cave painting – cool . . .

I drew me and Celeste on the cupboard door with a jammy heart round us. I drew Mum on her own – and made her look like a crazy troll. Then I crossed her out. I didn't draw Toadstool because he was just too disgusting to even draw.

I don't know how long we were mucking about like that. But Celeste was cooing happily and splatting jam on the floor when the front door banged.

I jumped.

Mum? Was she back already?

I caught my breath suddenly. Looking about at what I'd done . . .

Oh no. What HAD I been thinking?

The kitchen was completely and utterly wrecked. Everything was upside down, dripping, ripped and broken. Even the ceiling was covered with splat and goo . . .

I'm going to be blinking FOR IT.

Oh God, Mum would be angrier than she'd ever been in my whole life. And shocked. Because I was normally so good.

Not any more . . .

My heart boomed with panic.

But a tiny hope began creeping through me

too. Maybe – just maybe – Mum was back early because she'd had a final, big bust-up with Scummy Scott.

Oh, please let that be true. Make him be gone forever . . . .

I closed the kitchen door behind me, and picked my way through the boxes in the hall. I pulled the front door open a crack.

It was just the postman.

With some silly parcel for Toadstool.

I took the parcel and closed the door, breathing hard.

Mum wasn't back, then. How stupid to think she might be . . .

I started clambering back over the boxes to the kitchen. But I was so busy thinking about Mum that I stumbled and knocked an old shoe box off one of the piles.

Its lid came off and stuff tipped out onto the carpet.

Photos.

And a necklace.

I picked it up. It was very delicate and must

have been quite old as the silver chain had gone black. I turned it over in my hand.

A purple butterfly. Made out of pretty stones.

Another purple butterfly! They're just everywhere . . .

I slipped it into my jeans pocket, and picked up a handful of photos. I never got to see old photos because Mum wasn't big on having pictures up in frames that needed dusting.

I couldn't remember ever even seeing these ones. And they were so funny! There was one of me and Mum making snow angels in the garden, and another one of us two playing Barbies – both when I was about four. Then one taken on my first day at school, with Mum hugging me in my uniform, looking proud.

Me and Mum.

Me and Mum.

All smiles. And all taken before Toadstool came stinking along.

Happy days . . .

I picked up another handful of photos, and stared at the one on top.

And gasped.
A baby gazed back at me.
No . . .
But it really was . . .
It was Celeste.

Chapter Twenty

I sat on a box, gawping at the photo.

I held onto it with both hands, and looked and looked and looked. I had to blink to make my eyes work enough.

There was no mistake.

It was her.

Same tufty, honey-coloured hair and cheeky toddler grin. And – oh my God! – the Celeste in the photo had on that little rabbit suit – the same one as Celeste was wearing in the kitchen, now all covered in choccy and gunge.

Why is there a photo of her in our cupboard?!
There were words on the back.

In Mum's loopy writing, it said: *Shell, fourteen months old.*

Shell . . . ?

I looked back at the baby in the picture.

It was me.

Baby me.

And it was Celeste.

Uh?

So is Celeste, like, ME when I was a baby?

Did she fly here from eleven years ago?

Only the eyes were different. In the photo, my baby eyes were bluey-green. Celeste had those strange, lavender eyes.

I catapulted into the kitchen to look at Celeste. She was rocking on her bottom in her rabbit suit, singing, and drawing jammy worms on the cupboard door.

Or I was.

Me.

I started shaking.

This can't be happening!

I dropped the photo, and backed out of the kitchen.

I felt suddenly sort of scared of Celeste.

How can she be me? I must be mad. Really, properly mad.

Somehow it had been fun when she was my magic, fairy baby, but this was like real mad people's stuff.

I thought of the library book. And that word – 'disturbance'.

They lock disturbed people up, don't they?

I felt faint and I swayed on my feet.

'Oh, Mum!' I cried.

To no one.

Then I scrambled over the stuff in the hall, stuffed my feet into my flip-flops, and took off out of the front door and away.

I left her by herself.

Left. Me. By myself.

Chapter Twenty-one

I had no idea where I was going. I stumbled along anywhere. My eyes were blurry. I tried opening and closing them, but all I could see was Mum's face, all mixed in with Celeste's little screwed-up face, crying and crying for me . . .

MY face. MY little face.

'You OK, Shelley?'

I turned. It was my old dinner lady, Mrs Denning. She was looking at me really funny.

I suddenly came to. I could feel my face was wet with tears and still half-plastered with dry, cracking chocolate. I'd forgotten . . . I still had my chocolate make-up on. Outside. In the street.

I must have looked like a mentalist.

Because I am one.

Without answering Mrs Denning, I trotted away.

I rubbed as much of the chocolate off as I could. Then I pulled the hood of my hoodie up, tugged my hair over my face, and just followed my feet.

I didn't know how I ended up near the Rec.

There were lots of people about suddenly – even though it was evening. So much music and light and noise. Of course . . . the bank holiday fair was there. I went in the gate and stood panting as people brushed past me. The smells made my tummy turn – dirty engine fumes, hot sugar and popcorn – and the roar of the rides pounded in my head. I couldn't hear myself think.

Good! I don't want to think.

But the thoughts kept pushing through.

Celeste.

Super tiny.

Fairy baby.

I knew I had been premature when I was born. In one of those fish-tank cots. And so teeny-weeny.

That's why she was so small.

Because I was small.

Because she's me.

It was too much.

I elbowed my way to the front of the queue for the loudest, fastest ride I could see – the Wall. When the ride man wasn't looking, I nipped into a seat without paying. People shouted at me, but I blanked them. I strapped myself in next to a big lad who said something to me, but I shook my head at him and looked away. I just wanted to be whirled and turned and spun super fast so my brain would be jelly and wouldn't work.

I closed my eyes tight as it began. It went fast straight away. My head was flung backwards and my whole face juddered and rippled. The ride went faster and faster till everyone was screaming and I screamed too. Screamed and screamed and screamed.

'All right?' asked the lad as the ride slowed to a stop. I nodded, but it was a lie.

I staggered off the ride, feeling dizzier than ever. The sweet stall was right in front of me. Normally I was mad for that stall, but now all the sweets looked extra pink and gooey. The sickly smell clagged in my mouth, and made me feel like puking.

Sick, sick, sick . . .

The world was still going round, turning and turning and turning like the Wall. I wandered around the fair, bumping into people but not even caring. And then out onto the streets, going nowhere but just walking and walking as the evening got darker. It was windy and spitting with rain, but I was boiling hot. Then cold. Then hot again. I started sneezing again. My throat felt raw and scratchy, and my head was cah-booming so much I had to keep closing my eyes.

Of course I fell. Tripped over my own flip-flop.

Owww!

Blood seeped through the chocolate on my hands, and I could taste blood in my mouth.

The hurt was almost good for a moment. It made me feel properly there.

Instead of living in cuckoo land with a baby who is me.

I scrambled up onto a low garden wall. I lay down on it to try and feel less sick.

Mum . . . help me.

I suddenly wanted her more than ever. For her to tell me everything was OK. That I wasn't going mad. For her to make everything all better.

I wobbled to my feet. I would go home and phone her straight away.

I felt in my pockets for my keys.

Not there . . .

Of course – they were behind the blinking radiator.

I was locked out. And my phone was locked in.

But I have to phone Mum!

I stood there, all dopey, not sure what to do. Until my eyes landed on the hotel opposite. The hotel where Mum worked. Some of them knew me in there.

I crept in.

Jill the cleaner was hoovering out front.

'All right Shelley, love,' she said, turning off

the hoover. 'How's your ma? Better?'

Of course, Mum was off sick. Pretending.

'Yes, getting better,' I said. My voice sounded funny to me. Gratey. 'But I lost my phone . . . and my keys . . . and my mum's not answering the door. Could I just use your phone to tell her?' I felt faint with trying to talk properly.

'Yeah, sure, go in the back office, no one's in there. And take care, love. You look a bit peaky yourself.' She started the hoover up again.

I shut the office door behind me.

I knew Mum's mobile number off by heart. She'd made me learn it.

Answerphone.

After the bleep, words just poured out of me, all joined up.

'Mum, please come home. I'm poorly . . . I don't know what to do! Everything's so horrible. You don't look after me any more. You only think about HIM. It's like I don't even have a mum.' The room seemed to be fading in and out. I gabbled even faster, gulping back tears. 'Why have you gone without me? Why d'you always have to be

156

on Scott's stupid side? He's mean to me, Mum. You don't even know. He pretends to be nice, but he wishes I wasn't even born. He . . . he . . . he . . .'

I slammed down the phone. And then immediately picked it up and dialled again, breathing hard. This time I yelled . . .

'If you love Scott more than me, why don't you just put me in the bin, Mum? You only care about him. NOT ME! I hate him. And I HATE YOU!'

I slammed the phone down again.

I was trembling. From head to foot.

I couldn't believe I'd yelled at Mum like that. I'd said everything I'd been thinking for so long – all in one go. Just like that.

It felt like the moment after you jump off the top of the Death Slide at the adventure park – just falling into nothing. My legs folded up under me and I sank to the floor.

She'll never forgive me for what I said. Now she'll never come back. She'll stay with Toadstool in Birmingham.

I reached up, snatched the phone, and pressed redial.

My eyes filled so it was like looking up from the bottom of a pool. Tears choked me.

'M-m-mum, s-s-orry,' I choked. 'M-m-mummy, p-p-please c-c-come . . . I'm s-s-cared.'

The hoover noise stopped, and Jill came in. I dropped the phone and pulled myself to my feet by the desk.

'You all right?' She saw my face. 'You crying?'

I nodded, gulping. 'Fe-e-el poorly. G-g-going now.' My words came out like a broken robot.

I limped past her, and across the hotel reception to the exit.

'Shelley!' Jill called after me. 'Promise me you'll go straight home and find your mu—' I pushed the door shut on the word.

I walked again. In circles around the streets. I felt so odd and foggy – like I was doing big wobbly steps into nothing, moonwalking style. I wanted to go home so much, but I couldn't. Not unless I broke a window to get in.

I'm in enough trouble with Mum already.

Then I had a thought.

Jay's.

It wasn't far to Jay's house, but it felt like miles.
I rang the bell.

No one.

I knocked and knocked.

Nothing

They weren't in.

I knocked once more, then I slumped down onto their doorstep in a huddle. It was really peeing down, and the wind gusted, sharp in my ears. I could hear the sea, whipped up and angry, far away, smashing on the pebbles.

And a whining noise . . . At first I thought it was just the wind, but then I knew what it was.

Celeste.

Crying and crying. It was her newborn cry – she must have shrunk back to her teeny-tiny self.

Inside the house.

In JAY'S house?

It was like she was actually following me.

Of course she is. She's you . . .

A winding pain twisted sharp and hot in my ear. I nearly chucked up.

It was all too much. Too mad. But still I felt like

I had a magnet inside me, pulling me to Celeste. I couldn't help it – I wanted to bang down their door to get to her, and comfort her.

All on her own in there. Crying for her mum.
Me crying.
For Mum.
Mum . . .

I dragged myself half to my feet.

Dumb idea.

I was too woozy. The world tipped and I crashed down hard on top of their metal dustbin.

For a moment I tried not to breathe, so the pain would stay away. But then it came – ripping through my tummy and side. I lay in a heap for ages, gasping. Then somehow I dragged myself back into the doorway. I pulled my hood right down over my face and slumped low against the door. My head whirled.

Mum, please come back . . . I need you.

A million cars went past and past and past on the big road. The rain pelted on. And on. And on.

I curled up tighter. Into a small, wet ball in the dark. My teeth chattered.

Too hot.

Too cold.

The rain drummed right through my soaking hood.

Black . . .

Chapter Twenty-two

I woke up in a bed.

Not my bed.

And I was wearing someone else's huge T-shirt.

Where am I?

The sun was still shining outside the curtains, but the room was dark and hot and still. I had to gasp fast to get enough air. My heart was beating in my throat.

Celeste's crying filled my ears. I could feel her next to me, squirming in her restless sleep. Her little body felt boiling and damp against me.

I opened my eyes wide and tried to suss out where I was.

Boxes everywhere. Clothes that weren't mine.

My head dipped and spun.

Celeste squawked louder.

I rubbed her back weakly, but my head felt like a scraped-out boiled egg, and my skin prickled. My mind filled slowly with what had happened. What I knew.

Mum has gone. Celeste . . . is me.

Oh God . . . you're me . . .

And the messages. Oh no, the messages! Now Mum probably hates me . . .

Celeste's crying got louder. An alarm in my head. Heat swept up me. The room seemed to be rocking, so I closed and opened my eyes to make them work better.

Where AM I?

There was a box on top of the wardrobe.

One for the Pot. That funny game . . .

Jay's . . .

Of course. I was at Jay's. This was her room. Her bed.

I was half trying to sit up when something landed with a thump on my tummy, knocking me back flat. My face was covered with tiny licks.

It was Winnie the Poodle.

He lifted my duvet with his nose, and snuffled down under it with his bottom sticking out.

Celeste was still under there. Scriddling in her sleep.

Winnie's tail started waggling like mad.

Can he see her?

He popped his head out, and did a yappy spin on top of me.

A loud voice: 'Oi, Winnie, get out now!'

Winnie leapt off the bed and scarpered.

A figure appeared above me.

It was Jay.

'All right, sicko,' she said. 'Awake now?'

'What . . . why am I . . . ?' It tore my throat to talk.

'Why are you here? Aha, well . . . cos I saved you! We found you half-dead on our doorstep – all covered in dirt and soaking wet. My dad carried you up here.'

'I don't remember . . . '

'Nah, you never woke up properly – you were so done in. Not even when I helped you change out of your soggy clothes into Dad's old T-shirt.'

I sort of remember that now . . . like a dream.

'Thanks . . .' I croaked.

'No probs. But obviously you owe me big time for saving you! And letting you have my bed. It's gonna cost.'

I could tell she was joking around a bit to cheer me up. I tried to smile, but my face felt dead and sort of spongy.

Too hot. Too hot. Too hot.

Jay sat on the bed, squashing my feet.

'How you doing now?' she asked, gently.

'Ummmm,' I murmured. 'Fine.'

'Yeah, course,' she said. 'You look so fine. Well, don't worry, we'll look after you. Dad's just nipped to yours again to see if your mum's home yet. He put a note through your front door about an hour ago to say you're here, but she hasn't rung yet.' Her words bumpity-bumped around my head, but I couldn't get much sense out of them. 'Anyway, Dad says you got to have a drop of water to cool you down. And I got you some jelly snakes, look . . .'

Her voice echoed and whined through the room. It mixed up with the drilling buzz-buzz of a fly that bumped again and again against the window.

She ripped open the sweet bag. The noise crackled into my ears and made Celeste startle.

'Best test them out for you, eh?' she said, thickly. I looked up at her. Sugar glistened round her lips, sticking them together. The smell of the jelly snakes hit me – sickly sweet like gone-off fruit. My whole mouth filled with spit.

Horrible sweets.

I rolled away, swallowing hard. My face felt red-hot even though I was shivering. The colours of the duvet looked too bright and churned inside my head – nasty colours, pond green, fishy orange, puke yellow . . .

'BOWL!'

Jay stuffed her bin under my face just in time. I lay back after, trying to breathe.

Some of the sick had gone on the sweet bag.

'Uh-oh,' said Jay. 'Yeah, Dad did say I shouldn't give them to you.'

I just closed my eyes.

Chapter Twenty-three

My sheets felt wrinkled and hard, and I tossed and turned, burning up and freezing.

Celeste was there. And then she wasn't. And then she was. Little, red, lollipop face screaming. Tiny body, hot as a jacket potato next to me. Sighing, whimpering . . .

Or was it me?

But she is me . . . .

Not that I cared any more. I was too ill to worry about being mad. It was just lovely to have her there.

I rocked and sang to her. But not out loud, just in my head.

Because she can still hear . . .

'Silent Night . . . all is calm, all is bright.'

I twirled her hair, and my hair. It calmed her a little.

Calmed us.

Two shapes in the dark. Jay and . . .

Mum? Please be Mum.

'Hi, Shelley, it's Mark, Jay's dad.' His voice was soft. 'We got to get your temperature down, sweetheart. Come on, have a little sip.' He made me drink some water, and gave me a spoonful of pink medicine. Then he laid a wet flannel on my hot forehead. Really gently.

He's so kind.

'Shelley, do you know where your mum is?' he whispered. 'I even asked some of your neighbours, but no one seems to know.'

I kept my eyes closed.

She hasn't come because she hates me now.

'Can you think where she might be? Has she gone somewhere . . . with your baby sister?'

Baby sister!

I screwed my eyes tighter.

'OK, don't worry. I know you're feeling rotten. I expect she'll be home soon and see the note. You sleep now.'

I rolled my face into my pillow and stayed there until I heard him creep out.

'He's gone now,' came Jay's voice, after a while. 'My dad, I mean.'

I rolled back over.

She was lying on her floor next to the bed, reading a footie mag. 'So now you can tell me where your mum is. I promise I won't squeak to Dad.' She shrugged. 'Because obviously you know, where she is, don't you . . .'

I nodded. It made my brain rattle to move my head. 'Yeah, she's gone moping after her scabby ex-boyfriend to try and get him back. Birmingham or somewhere in his van.'

'So she doesn't know you're here.' She sat up and looked at me.

'No, she thinks I'm at my other friend's house. I did leave her a message saying I felt ill. But she hasn't come.'

Hasn't come . . .

'Well, Birmingham's a long way away . . .' said Jay.

'But I said horrible things to her on the message – I said I hated her!' My nose was fizzing and I was swallowing hard. 'It's just that she's been mental since Scott left her, see – like proper cracked up . . . and I can't cope if Scott comes back to live with us. He's so mean.'

'Rough,' said Jay. 'Poor you.'

My eyes and nose were running. For a moment I thought I heard Celeste start wailing. I felt for her, but she wasn't there.

'You can always come here . . . any time you want,' said Jay. 'Dad likes you . . . and anyhow, you've made yourself so at home, chucking up everywhere, you're practically my sister now!'

Even though my head was killing me, I could tell she meant it.

Thank you . . .

She squeezed my hand, and I fell back into a jaggedy sleep.

Chapter Twenty-four

'Who's Celeste?'

My eyes pinged open.

I was dripping with sweat and the room looked all wavy.

'You don't half chat on in your sleep – it's been better than telly, actually.'

Jay was still there on the floor, with her laptop open on some game.

'You were on about Celeste . . . who's she?'

I nodded. 'She's a baby.' It came out like a squashed whisper.

'Your sis?'

I shook my head, and the walls wobbled.

'No . . .' I paused. 'A baby . . . that only I can see.' My voice sounded odd and slurry.

I strained in the half-light to see Jay's face.

Why am I telling her? She won't believe me.

But I was too weak to worry. And she didn't laugh at me. I could see she was thinking hard about what I said.

Might as well give her the punchline . . .

'And the baby is ME,' I whispered.

'You?'

'Yeah, baby-me. She's been coming this week when I've been upset, and I've looked after her . . . well, looked after me! It's been dead weird.'

Jay sat thinking for a moment. Like she was trying to joggle my words into ones she could understand. Then she nodded.

'Epic,' she said 'It's a bit like real-life Dr Who. I wish that would happen to me.'

I don't know if she really believed me, but I could see she wasn't taking the mickey.

'So you don't think I'm off my trolley then?'

She made a cross-eyed, crazy face.

'Well, yes, obviously you're mad as a carrot . . . and that's why I like you.'

Chapter Twenty-five

'Shelley – it's Dr Brent here.'

I came to, aching from head to foot.

Dr Brent?

Oh yes, she was that doctor me and Mum saw at the surgery. I didn't like her much – she always spoke to me in this bright voice like I was five and stupid.

'Just going to have a little listen to your chest. 'Is that all right?' She put the metal circle of her ear thing on my chest, and listened to my breathing. It felt icy even through my T-shirt.

Then she looked in my ears and put a thermometer under my tongue. She chattered on about kiddy telly programmes I never watched.

I didn't answer her like I usually did, all polite like a goody-goody. I wanted her to leave me alone. Leave us alone. My head was sore, and Celeste was squeaking in her sleep, her face scrunched up and red.

I closed my eyes and pretended to be asleep again.

I want Mum . . . not you!

The doctor went and stood by the window for ages, whispering to Jay's dad. Their voices were muffly, but I heard some words – 'fever', 'virus', 'stress', 'mother', and then 'baby sister', 'imaginary' . . .

Imaginary! Had Jay told her dad about Celeste? No. It was that doctor – she knew I didn't have a sister.

The doc will think I'm a head case . . . give me some mad pills.

The doctor was coming back across the room.

I hugged Celeste to me, and pulled the sheet

right up over our heads.

'Shelley.'

I felt her hand on the duvet.

'Get off,' I croaked. My tongue felt fat and useless in my mouth.

'Just pop your head out for a minute, Shelley, love,' she said.

'No!'

And Celeste roared too. And grew. Grew into her big toddler size in one second flat.

She threw off the duvet, grabbed the wet flannel and flung it at the doctor.

'NOOOOOooooooooooooooo!' She knocked my glass of water all over the bed.

I looked up to see the doctor's shocked face. Sorry for me. And worried.

Maybe she'll take me away . . . Put me in a home . . .

'Mum! I just want my mum!' I wailed. 'Why isn't she coming?'

Chapter Twenty-six

Crazy, looping, turning dreams. Minutes or hours melting together. The curtains stayed drawn. Mark crept in once and gave me more pink medicine, but I got hotter and hotter. The fly – or was it that butterfly? – bumped against the window again, again, again, forever. I thought Celeste was next to me some of the time, although I wasn't even sure any more. But I could always hear her . . . crying inside my head, on and on.

Then someone was there.

A cool hand on my hot cheek. I tried to open

my eyes, but it was like I was looking through water. I could hear voices a long way away. All muddled and droning – strange, twisted sounds, stretched-out, long sounds, all mixed up.

Celeste got louder.

'MUMMM! MMUMM!'

She was crying from inside me.

Like it was actually me.

Actually me.

'MUM-M-M!'

'Shelley! I'm here, darling! Shelley – open your eyes.'

Mum?

I blinked through my tears.

Mum?

It WAS Mum. Really Mum. Standing next to my bed. In true life.

She'd come.

I flew up into her arms and clung round her neck. She sat down, and I curled up small on her lap, and sobbed. Howled and howled. It was the first time I'd cried like that since forever.

She just kept rocking me. For ages and ages.

Rocked me into a heavy blank sleep where no more dreams came.

Chapter Twenty-seven

Mum stayed with me all night, squished up in Jay's little single bed. I snuggled into her and we listened to faraway seagulls and the rain plinking at the windows.

We slept. For hours and hours.

It felt like all the clocks in the whole, entire world had stopped ticking.

Celeste wasn't there any more, but I could hear her little noises. Breaths and happy sighs. Soft, soothing sounds.

Quiet, close, inside, safe.

Chapter Twenty-eight

I blinked into morning sunshine and stretched. My head felt like I had a motorcycle helmet on – thick and slow and heavy. But my hotness had gone and I didn't feel sick.

Mum . . .

It's real, isn't it? She's back . . .

I looked around the room. My clothes were all folded up on Jay's chair in a neat-freaky pile.

Yep, only Mum would do that.

The old Mum anyway . . .

The window was open, and a soft sea breeze

flapped at the curtains. The air smelt fresh and good. I could see a slither of sky – clear and blue like it had been washed clean by the rain.

I got up stiffly and shuffled next door to the loo.

I looked at myself in the mirror.

What a ragbag. I looked thin, and my hair had matted itself into a Mr Whippy whirl on top of my head.

Mr Whippy whirl?

That was Celeste's hairdo. I stared at myself again. Blimey, I really did look like Celeste.

I jumped as a plastic tube poked round the door.

'Hands up!' Jay pushed in, pointing a super-soaker water pistol right at my head. 'Aww, no, you're better, aren't you,' she said. 'I was looking forward to cooling you down, but looks like I'm too late. Bum!'

I grinned and stuck out my tongue at her.

'Your mum's downstairs, by the way – chatting on to Dad,' she said, following me back into her room.

'God, your dad's been so nice letting us stay here.' My voice sounded broken up and creaky.

'Me, sicking up all over the place . . . then Mum coming and staying too. And you don't even know us.'

'Well, we were hardly gonna throw you both out in the middle of the night, were we? And like I said – you can come here any time, SIS.' She grinned. 'Just remember to bring doughnuts as your entry fee next time.'

'Knock, knock!' Mum looked in. 'Heard your voice.' She was wearing some blue pyjamas that were too short for her – she must have borrowed them from Jay. She looked skinny in them, and so tired.

'See you in a bit,' said Jay, cheerfully. She winked at me and left.

Mum perched on the bed. She looked shy. 'How you feeling?' she said. 'Not so hot?'

I shrugged. 'Bit better . . .'

Yes, I really am.

But I avoided her look and scowled. Somehow, now I was awake, I felt angry with her all over again.

Tears prickled the back of my eyes.

For a moment I thought I heard Celeste whimper in my head.

I twirled my hair and took deep breaths.

Calm . . .

'I'm sorry, baby.' Mum's voice quivered. 'I didn't get your messages until we got to Birmingham – I didn't hear my phone go off in the van. But I came as soon as I listened to them. Oh, Shells, I'm just so sorry about . . . well . . . just, everything!' She gathered me into her arms 'You were so right about Scott, and I was so stupid. I just didn't see it. It was like I was under his spell or something,' she said grimly. 'He hardly spoke to me on the van journey. I don't even know why he let me come. He only opened his mouth to ask if he could have Fuzz-wuzz!'

'You're not letting him!' I cried.

'No! Of course not. And then when I wanted to drive straight home because you were ill, he got really nasty. He said he couldn't "deal with my child", and all this mean stuff about you. I was so shocked! I just got out of the van at some traffic lights. But he parked up and came after me, shouting about how it's over forever because he's got another girlfriend. Then he asked for his stuff back. The cheek! I just kept walking. It took ages to find the station, but I got the train home.'

She sighed and sniffed.

'Honestly, the train wouldn't go fast enough. Of course I went straight to Lexi's, but no one was in. Then I found Mark's note at home and ran here. He said you've been really bad – sick and hallucinating. Poor baby.'

Hallucinating? That's, like, seeing stuff that isn't there . . .

She must mean about Celeste . . .

Mum was still talking. 'I'm so sorry, Shelley. I know I've been, like, 100% rubbish.'

I wiped my wet face on my sleeve. I hadn't even known I was crying – I was getting so good at it now.

'Can you forgive me?' She gazed at me sadly through her long lashes.

Long like Celeste's.

'Yes . . .' I began. And then I stopped.

Do I mean that?

Or was I just being her good girl again?

'Yes-s-s . . .' I said slowly, ' . . . but only if you don't get any more horrid boyfriends!'

And I *really* meant that.

Chapter Twenty-nine

Mum stayed with me for a while, lying next to me on the bed. I couldn't believe how tired I was seeing as I'd just laid in bed for so long. But Mum said that happens when you're ill.

'Oh yes,' she said, sitting up like she'd just remembered something important. She reached for something on the bedside table. 'Where did you find this?! I was amazed to find this in your jeans – I haven't seen it for years.' She dangled the purple butterfly necklace in front of my nose.

'I found that in the hall – in a box of photos.'

Photos of me.

Celeste.

I half wanted to tell her all about Celeste then – blurt it all out – but I just didn't know where to start. And she stopped me short –

'Your dad bought that for me.'

Wow – a present from my dad. She had me listening then.

'My dad? When? When he was down here?'

I knew some stuff about him. He came from up north, and he and Mum had met when he was on holiday with his family in Lunham-by-Sea one summer. They were young, but they had a fling, and then that was it – there I was.

Mum nodded and smiled, all misty.

'He was such a good-looking boy, you know – very nice and kind too. Just way too young to cope with being a daddy. He didn't know what had hit him, poor love. And his family were not impressed. So in the end we kind of lost touch. Except for the odd cheque.'

I'd heard some of this before.

'Nice and kind . . . that's not really your type

is it, Mum,' I said, grinning at her a bit cheekily.

She sighed. 'Well, you're not wrong there, Shells.'

And then very carefully, like it was so precious, she fastened the butterfly necklace around my neck.

My skin tingled where it touched.

Chapter Thirty

Later, Jay and Mark bowled into the room, giggling like wallies. Mum followed in behind.

'Look what I made you,' said Jay.

It was a green pig. Carved out of kiwis and stuck together with cocktail sticks. It had red jelly tots for eyes.

'That's one ugly, angry pig,' I said.

Jay leant over and whispered in my ear. 'He's called Scott.'

We sniggered.

'Yeah, it was Dad's idea to make you fruit

animals,' gabbled Jay. 'He said you need the vitamins. Show her yours, Dad . . . pah, ha, ha!'

Mark's was basically just a heap of banana and orange pieces. 'It's supposed to be an elephant,' he said, sitting down on the end of the bed and fiddling with the fruit. 'But I admit it looks more like a squashed jellyfish.'

Mum smiled at him. Just a smile. But it set off a little alarm in my head.

I looked at her sharply. And kept staring at her. Checking she wasn't fluttering her eyelashes, or giving Mark any of her girlie looks.

Because, seriously, I wouldn't have put it past her to start looking for a new boyfriend straight away.

Not that Mark was her type – he was way too nice. But nice or not, I could not deal with it if she got a new bloke ALREADY.

But I was panicking over nothing.

I watched Mum as she beamed at Jay too, as they tried to make the dappy fruit elephant stand up.

Then Mum reached down and pulled a huge

box of posh choccies out of a bag at her feet. 'I got them for you both,' she said, handing them to Mark. 'As a BIG thank you.'

She smiled at him again. Just a friendly, grateful smile, I was pleased to see.

It didn't take Jay long to get the box open. Everyone else had one, but the sugary smell made my nose wrinkle. It reminded me of sicking up.

Mum noticed.

'You off the sweet stuff now, Shells?' she asked.

'Ugh, yeah,' I said. 'I think maybe forever.'

'You – off sweets forever! Blimey, that's a turn-up,' said Mum. 'It's all change round here, seems!' And she smiled at me, still quite shy.

I smiled back, a bit shy too.

Yeah, all change . . . I hope.

'No probs, I'll have yours,' said Jay. And stuffed two chocs in her mouth at once.

Chapter Thirty-one

Mum went home to clean up. I knew she must've been so shocked at the mad mess in the kitchen when she'd gone home the night before. But she hadn't told me off or anything.

I still felt a bit weedy so Mum said I could I stay at Jay's for the afternoon and watch telly with her.

Mum came back for me in the evening. I gave her a big hug.

It was lovely and warm out.

'How about a chip picnic on the beach?' she said, as we walked home.

Blimey, Mum never eats fat food like that . . . At the chippy Mum ordered two lemonades and two chips with loads of pickled-onion vinegar and salt.

Slugface rode past the chip shop. He saw me, but he just looked down and carried on.

Ha!

While we waited, Mum chatted to the chip shop man. Then she started giving him the old eyes-and-smiles treatment, and giggling for no reason. This time I wasn't imagining it. She really was doing her flirty thing.

I scowled.

I knew it! She can't help herself, can she? And this one IS her hairy-ape type . . .

When the man turned away to the till, I nudged Mum and shot her my evil-est look. I pointed at him and mimed cutting my throat with my hand. 'Just no! Leave him alone,' I said under my breath. 'No boyfriends!'

Her smile vanished and she went pink. 'What? I'm not doing anything!' she mouthed back.

'Yes you are,' I whispered, and gave her another dirty look. *I'll strop and shout. Like Celeste!*

The man handed us our chips over the counter.

'There you go, lovely ladies,' he said.

Mum didn't giggle again. She just turned and hurried out of the shop without even saying goodbye to the chip man.

I followed her out.

She was stood on the corner waiting for me, scuffling her feet and chewing her lip. She looked at me like a told-off dog. 'OK, Shell, fair cop in there,' she said, quietly. 'You caught me.'

We walked along the street a bit in silence. 'And you're right.' she said. 'I hate not having a bloke . . . but I got to keep away from men for a while. I'm no good at them!'

'You can say that again,' I said. 'And I really WILL go and live at Jay's house if you choose another rank one.'

'Phew – get you, chopsy!' said Mum, laughing. 'You got feisty, all of a sudden.'

I smiled and shrugged.

Yes, maybe I have . . . and it feels GOOD.

She linked her arm through mine. 'I think you and me got some catching up to do, haven't we.

Some serious "girl time" needed. I've not been a good mum to you recently, but I'm gonna make it up to you, just you see!'

We wandered over to the beach, still arm in arm, and found a small patch of sand. We sat close together getting damp bums, eating our hot tea out of the paper. After a while Mum got up and started searching the beach for shells and pebbles.

'Hey,' she said, 'this pebble looks like a wonky elephant.'

'With clogs on,' I giggled. 'Carrying a handbag.'

Then we both laughed our heads off. We just couldn't stop. Even though it wasn't that funny. We laughed and laughed and laughed.

We lay down on our jumpers. The traffic noise calmed to a swish, and the light faded.

Then I remembered something that had been niggling at me . . . I propped my head up on one elbow, so I could see Mum properly.

'Mum – did we ever have a cat called Bum?'

Mum's eyebrows flew into her fringe. 'Bum? Where did that question pop from? There's no way you can remember old Bum the cat!'

'Actually, I sort of do,' I said. 'Whose cat was she?'

'Our neighbour's . . . years back, when you were just a toddler. You called her Bum – although she was actually called Plum – and the name stuck, poor puss!' She shook her head. 'It's amazing you remember that – I'd nearly forgotten myself.'

'I loved Bum-cat,' I said.

'Yes, you did. Funny little baby, you were.' She kissed my hair. 'Such a sweetheart.'

'Yes, I was . . .' I said.

'Anyway, squish up, it's getting chilly,' said Mum.

I snuggled into her, and we lay listening to the whoosh of the waves. We watched the sky turn a soft milky-strawberry, and the sun melt into the sea. My fingers kept fiddling with the necklace round my neck, tracing the butterfly shape.

Lovely purple butterfly . . .

'Mum . . . do you think I could maybe see my dad one day?' The question just sneaked out, surprising me.

'Oh, Shelley!' said Mum, rolling onto her side to look at me carefully. 'Well, I always knew you might ask sooner or later.' She paused. 'Yes . . . I don't know where he is exactly, but I'm sure we can find out. It won't be easy, as we've lost touch, but I promise I'll try . . .' She stroked my hair out of my eyes, and her voice went softer. 'Then if we find him, we can talk again – and you can decide if you really do want to meet him. How's that sound?'

My dad . . .

I nodded hard.

She pulled me closer to her.

'I love you, Shells. Just so much.'

The moon came out, and then lots and lots of sparkly stars. Gulls kept flying past, making shadows across the sky – but I wasn't scared of them, lying there with Mum.

I took a peep at her in the moonlight – she looked so peaceful.

I thought of how I'd wished and wished that Mum would be Mum again.

Seemed like the spell had worked.

Celeste magic . . .

Oh, my little Celeste!

I wondered if I'd ever see her again – except in

baby pictures of myself. I didn't think so somehow
. . . she'd come to help me, and I was all right
now, wasn't I? So she'd gone back to being part
of me again.

It'd all been so totally weird.

And wonderful too . . .

'Wow, so many stars,' said Mum, reaching for
my hand. 'It looks like a huge firework went off
and froze in the sky.'

'Or angel eyes peeping down,' I whispered.

I put my arm up, and drew a big circle around
two stars with my finger.

My face.

Then I drew a smaller face right inside mine.

A little baby angel.

We were looking out of the same two
starry-eyes.

Then I gave us a great, big smile.

Acknowledgements

Heart-felt thanks to James Catchpole for your cleverness, sensitivity and endless patience. You are the bestest agent anyone could hope for.

Huge thanks to the wonderful Emma Matthewson and all at HKB for believing in my baby.

Thank you to Nicola Davies, Julia Green and my MA group at Bath Spa Uni for all your encouragement, back when Celeste was just a twinkle in my eye.

And thanks to my family for putting up with my pyjama-ed typing frenzies.